Insensible Loss

PAUL MICHAEL PETERS

Insensible Loss
Paul Michael Peters
ISBN 978-0-9891785-9-4

For Trina

Special thanks to

Brooke Payne
Nicole Ray
Jason Orr
Steven Bauer

"Sometimes eraser marks on a page mean more than what's written."
—Autor Widmor

Insensible Loss - medical: *the amount of water lost on a daily basis from the lungs, skin, and respiratory tract; the exact amount cannot be measured.*

Insensible Loss - wilderness survival: *unawareness that water loss is actually occurring; loss during high-intensity action simply breathed away, evaporated, and never realized.*

Contents

NODA

Year 2053
Olivia age 25

"**N**o one dies alone in this hospital," the doctor explained.
"What happened to him?" Olivia asked.
"He was flown in six hours ago from the city—struck by a vehicle and thrown several yards, or so I'm told. We did what we could for him in the ER, but we are not optimistic. The best we can do is keep him comfortable."

"Did he have anything with him? I.D.?" she asked.

"Here are his personals." He handed her a clear plastic bag. "There's a book in there. It looks like a really old family Bible from the leather binding. Might have a lineage or a name in it."

Removing it from the bag, she noticed that the soft leather in her hands felt like warm butter to the touch. Its pages, thin and worn, made it look ancient yet well cared for. Setting it down on a clean counter, Olivia put on a pair of purple latex gloves to handle it.

"Good call," the doctor said. "Wouldn't want to spoil it."

Looking through the pages, she asked, "Any relatives? Anything in the computer for contact?"

"The computer is working on it, and the police are searching, but they might not find anyone in time."

"There is little I can do," she said.

"It's good just to be with him. Let him know he is not alone," he said with reassurance.

Olivia entered his room. After her two years of serving in a hospital post–nursing school, she was accustomed to the beeps and whirs from the monitors. At first glance, he looked like nothing more than a lumpy pile of laundry on a bed needing to be folded and put away. Only his left eye, cheek, and mouth were exposed from the layers of gauze and wrap. He seemed stable enough breathing with an oxygen tube under his nose. The rise and fall of his chest was steady.

Olivia moved a comfortable chair to his bedside. She dug a little under the tightly tucked bedding to find his hand. From the liver spots, wrinkles, and veins, she could tell he was not a young man. Taking his hand in hers, she could also tell he was not a man of hard labor. "You are not alone," she said to him softly. "You are not alone."

Volunteering was a way to network with the staff at the hospital during the application process. Volunteering for No One Dies Alone, or NODA, provided a different perspective in care. As a nurse, there were so many checklists and rounds to fill her days that it was rare she spent long periods of time with the sick and injured. She had faced two types of people supporting loved ones. The first were willows, who swayed with any suggestion by the staff; they had bendable wills and few questions. Then there were the opposite, who always knew better, demanded details, and hovered over the patient like protective geese, honking warnings and commands. NODA introduced her to something more intimate. She needed to find a way to make a connection with the person through the layers of gauze, bandages, and tape. She tried to be a beacon one could find in the fog of drugs. As rewarding as this effort was, she still needed the full-time position.

"You are not alone," she repeated.

His eyelids began to flutter. "Morgana?" he gurgled.

With her free hand, Olivia pressed the call button.

"Morgana? Is that you?" he asked.

"My name is Olivia. You are in St. John's Hospital in the state of New York. It is June 27, 2053. Do you know your name?"

"Morgana, read me the book one more time," he said.

Olivia opened the book to look for an inscription or autograph. The title read "*The Ethics of Immortality* interpreted and transcribed by Autor Widmor." On the inside of the front cover lay two faint handwritten names, "Viktor Erikson" and "Morgana Erikson." Her voice was calm and hopeful. "What is your name, honey? That would be so helpful for us," she said.

"My name?" he started, his voice raspy and weak. "My name is Viktor Erikson. I was born to a family of fishermen on the fjords of Sweden."

"Your name is Viktor Erikson? This is your book?" She asked. She held the book up so he could see it. "Morgana Erikson is the other name here—is she your wife? Is she your contact?"

"Morgana?" he asked.

She added, "You don't sound Swedish. Have you been in this country long?" Taking a pen and paper from the desk beside his bed, she noted his words and the time. Behind her, she could hear another person.

"Morgana?" he muttered. "Read me the book one more time, Morgana."

Olivia turned to see the doctor. "He said his name is Viktor Erikson of Sweden. He keeps asking for Morgana." She handed the doctor the scribbled note.

"I'll notify the detective."

"He keeps asking for Morgana to read the book," Olivia said.

"Well, read him the book, I guess," he said.

Olivia watched the doctor exit the room in his brisk pace. She then looked down to the canonical gospel of Viktor Erikson and began to read aloud.

The Ethics of Immortality

interpreted and transcribed by Autor Widmor

Chapter One: Savannah

Year 1839
Viktor age 20
Morgana age 17

THE SAVANNAH SHIPPING yard of 1839 was awash in a deluge of new commerce now that the rail line connected the seaport to the city. Flags from warring nations fluttered above vessels unloading ballast, taking on cargo, and making the turn back out to sea.

One man did not care for king cotton, the slave trade, or spices. He was William Durand, the captain of the *Ponthieva*. The last provisions loaded, he needed only the two passengers that commissioned this expedition to board.

"Late in the morning to be setting sail, Captain," Erikson said. He had stood close so others nearby could not hear. His English was good and only carried a hint of the Swedish accent.

"Late indeed," he spoke low. "Our contractor and his guest are very late. Sail at first light, I told him. Nearly midmorning, and we are last in line to catch the tide," replied Durand.

"Who is this contractor?"

"Someone with gold in his pockets and little sense in the head. He has booked our services, insisting on little detail. Secrecy is the order of the day, Mr. Erikson. He was clear on this one point alone: not to speak of him or the expedition," he explained in suppressed volume.

Nearly half past ten, a gray-haired gentlemen dressed in social attire useless to the sea approached the dock with a woman on his arm.

"Good morning, Captain Durand," he called from the bottom of the plank. "Permission to board?"

"Aye," the captain called back.

The sweltering heat gathered on the brow and soaked the rim of the old man's collar. He made his way up the plank and over the side with delicate steps and the aid of the woman.

"Captain, allow me to introduce you to my daughter, Morgana."

"Ma'am," the captain said. "Now, if you could, please bid farewell to your father, take your leave, and be on your way. We must set sail."

"Oh no, Captain Durand, you are mistaken. You do not understand the situation. I am joining you and my father on this expedition of science," she said with a delicate Southern lilt. Her smile, flutter of the eyelids, and slight tilt of the head made for the small gestures of initial flirtation.

"Why the quibble, Captain? Our dealings were for two passengers. I am the first, my daughter the second," the doctor said.

The captain stepped close. "You said nothing of a woman, Dr. de la Motte, even one as fair and beautiful as your daughter, joining us. It is bad luck to bring a woman to sea. You must know this."

With a disjointed expression, the doctor replied, "Good Captain, this is a myth, an old wives' tale. There is no need to cling to this tradition."

"Like wearing traditional dress in the Georgia heat to board a ship?"

"Captain, good sir, I have traveled the globe with my father on expeditions. I have seen and done things no other woman has or ever may again. I assure you, I will not bring you bad luck . . . or slow you down." With a small and smart smile, she added, "You may even find it difficult to keep match with me."

The captain considered her for the moment. She was everything he disliked in his dealings with the indulgent Southern upper class. Her beauty was apparent; the putty color of her skin, her raven hair, and her ample bosom could stir life into the stricken man. At sea, her life was his duty and her safety his charge against savages and even his own men, if things turned. Durand was a man focused on the mission.

"I will take you on, hold true to the commission, but I must warn you, these are not easy days ahead. You are not passengers—you are part of the expedition, which means you, my dear, will be called on for duty, not be carried."

"I understand my place very well, Captain Durand, and accept those terms," she said.

"Mr. Erikson, call the men to deck," he commanded.

With a whistle blow and a bell ring, twenty-eight men stood at attention before the captain and first mate.

"Men," the captain's voice rang true across the deck. "As you know, we are taking on a commission for this next adventure. We are not military nor are we pirates; we are merchants, professionals all true. Has your trust in me has paid well?"

The men cheered, "Aye."

"Have I ever steered you wrong?"

The men cheered, "Nay."

"We are taking on a bold new venture south, an expedition of science and exploration. We are taking this man, Dr. de la Motte, and his daughter, Morgana."

There was a notable grumble from the deck at the suggestion of the fairer sex.

"His daughter," he repeated, "Ms. Morgana de la Motte."

Durand gave the men a long hard look they understood well. "We will treat them with the utmost respect. They are under my care and charge, and I will hold accountable any man, *any man*, who treats them differently."

There was an acceptance among the men. The captain had done them well in the past. He had saved many of their lives over the years, and they had been witness to the shaping of his legend for finding riches and treasure to return alive for spending.

"You won't lose your pants on this trip . . . maybe your life, but what's that?" The men laughed at the captain's grim humor. "Mr. Erikson, ready for departure."

Another whistle tone instructed the men to prepare for launch, weigh anchor, and hoist the sails. The crew of the *Ponthieva* was quick to take action as the doctor and his daughter watched from the captain's side. The ship moved into the fast currents and pushed away from the anchored vessels of the Cotton Exchange.

At the turn of the Tybee Island lighthouse, the *Ponthieva* pointed south, following the coast of Georgia down into Florida.

"We can push and make two hundred miles in a day when needed," Erikson said at the dinner table, his bandit smile full of confidence having lived one more day.

The doctor set his spoon down from the soup. Still dressed in his social attire, he looked uncomfortable in the heat. "Tell me, Captain, how did you come to command the *Ponthieva*?"

Durand politely forced a smile. "I would be more interested to discuss our final destination, Doctor, why you were late this morning to board, and why so much mystery in what we are doing. We are heading south, as you asked, but we could better prepare for this expedition of science knowing where the *Ponthieva* points her jib."

"*Ponthieva?* As in the flower?" Morgana inquired.

"Aye, it is," said the captain.

"More commonly known as the shadow witch?" she asked.

"Aye."

"What a clever name. Your ship is named after a rather beautiful orchid, but there is something deceptively *sinister* in the name as well."

"The captain is a complex man, Ms. de la Motte," Erikson said. "Ma'am, you are looking at the luckiest captain in all the Atlantic. Captain Durand won the *Ponthieva* in a game of chance in Asia." Erikson leaned in, capturing her attention. "This is not your average ship . . . it's an opium clipper."

"Opium?" She sounded surprised.

"She is fast and shallow, allowing our good captain to get us out of more than a few tight situations," Erikson explained.

"Don't let Mr. Erikson excite you. We are not pirates, we do not run opium for the crown, and I am a simple man focused on the expedition you have contracted. We need to know more to make this a success." The captain's voice was gruff and sounded like the gnarling of a bone, even in polite conversation.

There was something intriguing to Morgana about the captain's voice, about the command and the power that particular auditory effect produced. It bellowed from that hard and tough face, bitter like brine, clenched from staring at the sea, watching in wait. The "Yes, Captain" from Erikson was pleasing to her. Behind those deep and penetrating blue eyes was someone she could see herself with, something she could trust, even if it was masked by his devilish charm and smirk. There was something about this Viking she could not explain but wanted to explore.

"Still, an opium clipper, my word, that sounds dangerous," she said.

"It sounds like the perfect crew and experience we need for this expedition," the doctor said. "My apologies for being tardy, Captain, and for the secrecy too. We are heading south, past the tip of Florida to Mexico, just north of the Federal Republic of Central America."

"Revolution," the captain said. "Cholera. Local savages. The Spanish. What other reasons should I give you not to turn this ship around right now? Mr. St. Clair, could you ask Mr. Han and Mr. Turner to join us for dinner?"

The captain's third moved quickly from his seat and out the door as instructed.

"I trust you don't have a problem with blacks or the Chinese, because if you do, there are two more reasons I will turn back to Savannah."

"I have but one goal, sir. The methods used are irrelevant," the doctor said.

St. Clair returned to the cabin with the two men, whom the captain asked to join them at the table.

"This is Mr. Han, one of the best navigators I have ever had the pleasure to sail with." The captain pointed to an Asian man who was of solid build and carried himself confidently. "This"—the captain nodded in the direction of the black man—"is Mr. Turner." He was bald, lean, and athletic yet gentle. "Our boatswain and carpenter."

The doctor nodded to each of the men being introduced. The cook served the main meal, a mess of a dish which included some type of bird with vegetables and potatoes served from a single kettle.

"The good doctor was about to explain how important it is for us to travel to the Federal Republic of Central America despite the war, disease, and brutality."

Han quickly pulled out a small pad and a pencil to make a list of the responsibilities the captain would assign each man. Turner picked up his spoon to eat.

"I have spent my entire life, gentlemen, in the pursuit of knowledge for the improvement of the human life force. It is that thing inside each of us that makes us unique. Revivalists in the north will tell you it is a soul, something that one needs to cultivate with the heavens to protect from hell. I have met men in Europe who tell me that there is a collective responsibility of all human kind; our trust should be in the betterment of each other. Some have tried to explain that there is a magic or mysticism that is a greater power than our understanding which only a select few can command," he said, studying the reactions on faces of the men. "I will tell you there is *nothing* outside of our understanding with the proper study and observation."

"And what do we want to study?" St. Clair politely asked.

"It is the secret discovered and protected by the Maya for centuries of how to stay vital, healthy, and alive. It is the key to life eternal."

"The fountain of youth?" Durand asked skeptically.

"Some call it that. Others know it for what it truly is: an elixir of life that, when consumed, can change you to the very bone," he said.

"Gentlemen," the captain said, "we should prepare to turn back to Savannah after dinner. It seems that the doctor may need to be dropped off near a sanatorium."

"You don't believe me? That is fine. Set aside my purpose, forget the goal of *my* expedition, discount the *decades* of study I have spent on the matter, the maps I've discovered, and the evidence I have with me. Call the knowledge of this water or fountain a myth, if you must. Instead, consider the gold."

The eyes of the captain and crew grew large at the idea. Mouths began to water for more than food.

"Ancient, undiscovered treasures from centuries ago in lost cities that I have spent years designing a map to," he said with precision. "Maps that only I can interpret." He let the men in the room contemplate this concept. "Why are the Spanish so willing to give up lives by the thousands to march into a jungle infested with disease and overrun by savages? What could they be after? What do they know? What could they be searching for with an army of men?"

Eyes around the table moved from the doctor to the captain for a decision.

"They seek the very thing you want: gold . . . unimaginable treasures."

"I don't know. I can imagine a lot of treasure," Erikson was quick to quip.

"I have the map and the knowledge that will lead you there," the doctor replied.

In the silence that filled the room, the captain weighed the words of the doctor. "You have commissioned this ship for $500 a man to sail south for an expedition of science with another $1,000 a man for a successful return.

For that, you get the fastest ship with a seasoned crew. You still have a deal, doctor," the captain said. He spoke his intention down the table, "Mr. Han, I need you to chart the safest course down to the Yucatán. Work with the doctor on the maps he has. I want to avoid any major ports if possible. Stay away from those trap islands we found the last time and find a river outlet to lay anchor in so if we need to turn fast, we have a current with us. Mr. Turner, what do you know about Spanish ships?"

"They are formidable. Outnumbered and outgunned by the British, they would be more than a match for us. We would not be able to take on any ship; we would need to outrun them," Turner explained.

"Fine, my thoughts are the same. Rig for speed and maneuvering. We are going to have an advantage of hiding between islands or in the lee of a cove, not going gun for gun. We will need a few buckboards once we arrive to move heavy gold over soft soils," the captain instructed. "Mr. St. Clair, by the time we arrive, we should be running shallow. When we bring back the gold, we may need all the space in the hull. Inventory what we can throw over in case we need to make room fast."

"Aye, Captain."

The captain looked to his right. "Ms. de la Motte, what have you to contribute for us?"

"I am here at your pleasure, Captain," she replied.

"Mr. Erikson, Ms. de la Motte will assist you in the preparation of the expedition materials."

"Aye, Captain."

"How goes the watch, Mr. Erikson?" the captain asked.

"All's well," he replied. "It is a beautiful night—clear, calm, familiar waters."

"Tonight might be the last calm night we see."

With a tinge of playfulness, Erikson said, "I am looking forward to playing nursemaid to Ms. de la Motte on my duties the rest of the trip."

"What else is on your mind besides expensive women, cheap whiskey, and pure gold?"

"You just named my three reasons for living, Captain," Erikson said.

The captain flashed a smile. "You are the only one who can still make me laugh. What is really on your mind?"

"It's this fountain of youth folly, Captain. Have we become swash-bucklers? It is a myth."

"It's a straight deal. $500 a man for the trip, $1,000 on success. If we go there for mystic water and come back with dysentery, we are still making more on this trip than facing the North Atlantic in winter with a hull of rocks for ballast and cotton on the ride back."

"Ancient Mayan gold. It sounds too good to be true, especially from an old man and his daughter. There's another Spanish treasure nearby, a real treasure; the Atocha site is only three days from here. We can change course and start diving to retrieve real treasure, not promises."

"The Atocha site? Talk about folly. We could spend a lifetime trying to find her location and another bringing up the treasure. That cannot be the reason you are on the *Ponthieva*, Mr. Erikson," the captain replied. "We made an agreement with the good doctor."

"You made that agreement."

"And you gave your word to me."

"That is all I needed to hear, Captain. We are going through with this one hundred percent."

"If they didn't have a bounty on your head in Indonesia, we would be still running spices for the British."

"That admiral's daughter was worth it." The warm memory brought back a big smile to Erikson's face. "Beautiful, classy, and gutsy. Certain women have a way of changing boys into men and some men back into boys."

"Let's agree to keep the situation true with Ms. de la Motte. We do not fully understand what lies ahead."

"Aye, Captain," Erikson said.

"Still, there is a look she gives," the captain nearly sighed.

"Men into boys."

"You're right, Erikson. Best you and I don't vie for her attentions. Play it straight."

"Do I still get to look?"

"We both do."

∽ 3 ∾

Water

Year 2053
Olivia age 25

THE LITTLE TUNE from her mobile played. Olivia knew from the jingle it was her ex calling . . . again. He was persistent if nothing else. She had moved upstate to get away from him, away from her past. The first time, she could blame it on passion, the second may have been a mistake, but the third time he laid his hands on her that way was the end. She could not believe she had so quickly been deceived by him. He was so funny, so kind, and he knew how to be intimate. Still, he turned out to be like so many of the other men that had come in and out of her life over the years. She would not pick up or return any of his calls.

Olivia would have described it to her friends, if she had any, as feeling cursed. Each man in her life had brought a new item to her life to beat her with—this one literally, others with emotional ultimatums. It seemed that relationships were something to survive and recover from, like the flu, Ebola, or being hit by a truck. Relationships were not the area of growth, living, and replenishment so many of the "help" books she'd read described. She had once had a lover but could not risk another. This, more than anything, was the one thing she wanted: a partner, someone she would feel whole with.

This was the third "big move" in her life. There was no straight path she had been able to follow after leaving the Mennonite community in Pennsylvania, attending the public high school, and ending up here. It was the most courageous thing she had ever done to stand up not only to her mother and father but also to the elders in the community and declare that she would be leaving. If they were going to hold to the belief that men would be decision-makers to the abandonment of logic, the absolution of bad deeds would be handed out freely over broken bones, bruises, and other mental abuses, and there would remain things in the community that went "unspoken," she would be leaving. She would abandon their teachings and attend the public high school and then a state university. It was the start in a series of "best" decisions at the time. Following her first instinct to pursue the area of health care was the best of those choices. The two-year community college she started at in Pennsylvania transferred credits to the SUNY system in total. She was able to complete the four-year degree after the transfer and three additional years in the coldest location she had ever known off Lake Ontario. Then, she set her sights on a career where she could help and protect others.

South of that frozen wilderness of study, during her first year as a certified nurse, one of her peers told her about the best medical center in the state, if not the country, to work. St. John's was a small hospital in an influential area that had highly specialized doctors on staff who did not want to live or practice in Manhattan. It had been founded by an anonymous series of large donations in the 1890s. Each time the board of directors that managed the hospital asked for new facilities, new technologies, or additional research funds, they became available, as if it were nothing.

The most recent restructuring of the hospital had been ten years earlier, with very innovative ideas incorporated. It looked more like an airport in many ways than a traditional hospital. A long drive at the ground level for ambulances and drop-offs was reminiscent of the departure areas. Drop-offs would be greeted by a team at the "check-in" area that was isolated from other desks to control the spread of germs and diseases. Once a person was entered into the facility, a short period of isolation and decontamination would take place before moving to the test and examination areas that held the latest scanners and lab facilities. All of these systems were designed for the optimal routing and rerouting of information and patients to reduce the fatigue or miscommunication of the staff. Many of the world's leading experts would visit St. John's to study how the future of hospitals could impact the longevity and quality of life.

Olivia enjoyed the idea of working at the best and most advanced location. She wanted to be part of something great in her life after so many years of feeling the struggle to get ahead without forward movement. The interview process was different than others, more in-depth, longer. That is why she decided to volunteer with NODA, an accessible entry point into this world that might give her an edge or opportunity to impress the right person. There were two interviews she had passed and at least three more in her future if she were able to gain approvals.

That last hit had jolted something in her. She could not believe after having treated so many, after having been witness to the results of what placed so many in the emergency room, it had also happened to her, a smart and practical person. So when she decided to leave, she decided to move to something aspirational.

The room in which she watched over this dying man seemed more like a luxury apartment than a hospital. It was certainly nicer than her furnished rental. The chairs here were lush and comfortable. It hardly seemed a few minutes since she had started reading to Viktor, let alone the true two hours.

Viktor looked at Olivia with his one good eye. His voice was weak and scratchy. "Water," he said.

"Would you like some water? Are you thirsty?" she asked. Olivia went to the bathroom, filled a paper cup from the purified water spout, added a straw from that had been wrapped in paper protection, and returned to his side. She helped him with the straw and watched his lips purse and suck like a child's. She drew back the cup when he finished. He seemed to wait for something to happen, but nothing did. "You did a very good job, Viktor. Is there anything else I can get for you?"

His eye followed her movement, his black iris enlarged from the drip in his arm. "Who are you?"

"I'm Olivia. I'm here with you at the hospital. You are not alone."

"Where is Morgana?"

"Who is Morgana to you?"

"She is my life."

"Your wife?"

"Morgana?" he asked.

"I am Olivia."

"Read to me. Read the book, please," he said.

∽ 4 ∾

Chapter Two: *Ponthieva*

Year 1839
Viktor age 20
Morgana age 17

THE *PONTHIEVA* LOOKED worn from years of service. Above water, one could see the sun-bleached decks that had been scrapped and repaired repeatedly and the masts that seemed frail holding tattered sails. Below the waterline was an unexpected twenty-two-foot draft that could cut through the calm waters of the Mexican Gulf with great speed and ease. Turner had rig designs from the original ship build, giving the multiple sails greater area to capture the wind and shape them to carry the additional force that would normally bleed off into the forward canvas. His fast sails were slightly heavier than the normal, but the unique, rare oils that covered the canvas provided the combination of a flexible rigidity that untreated fabrics could not, giving the *Ponthieva* more control in following the slightest winds.

Looking over the port bow of the *Ponthieva*, Morgana watched the front edge cut through the waters and splash up the flare.

"Excuse me," she called to St. Clair.

"Yes, ma'am?" he obliged.

"What are those fish swimming with the boat?"

"Those are not fish, ma'am; those are dolphin. They are a sign of good luck for a ship. Very smart, they keep at our side. I have even heard stories of sailors' lives being saved after falling overboard."

Morgana's face turned. "They don't look very friendly with such a long nose. What is that hole on their head?"

"That is a blow hole, ma'am. That is how they breath."

"How do they taste? Do you catch and cook them?"

"Oh no, no, you wouldn't catch and eat them unless you were desperate."

"A dolphin steak might be delicious. Fry it in a pan?" she asked.

St. Clair shook his head. "I do not think you would want to eat one even if you could catch one."

"If I could catch one, I would bring it to the table . . . just for a taste."

"Pardon me, I need to return to my duties."

"You will not help me catch and kill a dolphin?"

"Only a witch would hatch such a plan for a sailor's comrade. No, thank you. That is very bad luck." St. Clair excused himself and returned to his tasks.

⟶⟫●⟪⟵

Another day ending and the last light fading into the distance, Erikson kept watch for light and movement across the horizon. His eyes had adjusted to the dark when she approached.

"Good evening, Mr. Erikson," she said.

"Ma'am."

"Are you enjoying the gloaming?"

"Yes, ma'am, thank you."

"What is it you are doing?"

Erikson looked to her and felt a chuckle at the question. "For you, it must look like I am standing here for my pure enjoyment. Just another pleasant evening aboard ship."

"Well, yes, isn't that what you are doing?"

"No, ma'am. I am standing watch. I am looking out across the horizon for lights from other ships, waiting for action on the ship, such as an emergency. I am watching out for my fellow sailors, ready to protect and provide assistance or a decision from the command." Erikson gave a sly smile. "But you already knew that from years of travel with your father."

She blushed and said with the Southern charm she'd displayed when boarding, "I may not carry all sophistication one presumes from a long lineage of travel. Passenger ships are a rather different experience. Do you mind if I stand watch with you?"

"No, ma'am, not at all. I welcome the notion." The edge of his lip curled with a devilish grin.

"Have you always been a sailor, Mr. Erikson?"

"I have been on the water since I was a wee boy. My mother was worried I might grow gills spending so much time on the fjords with Papa fishing."

"How did you come to sail on the *Ponthieva?*"

"My family took a steam ship to the United States. Some of my brothers became farmers in the Iowa territory, others lumberjacks in the territory of Wisconsin. But I loved the water—sailing is in my blood."

"But how did you meet the captain and join the crew of this shadow witch called the *Ponthieva?*"

"You wouldn't be interested in that tale."

"Oh, but I am."

"The first ship I worked was owned by a British merchant running spices from the East to colonies and up to the kingdom. They were lean years of hard labor with a mean scourge of a drunkard for a captain. One night on leave in Macau, I came across Captain William Durand in the back room playing faro. The odds were stacked against him. He had a lot of money on the table and was facing an angry man twice his size with six men watching his back." Erikson extended the glass in his hand and put it back to his eye to scan the horizon.

"Well, what did he do?"

"He won. Outnumbered, outgunned, and with everything on the table, he flipped his card and won straight out. Mr. Han and I were the only two in the room who covered Captain Durand as he collected the winnings—Han out of respect, but I was just impressed as hell one man would lay it all on the line like that." Erikson stopped. He took a moment with the glass to make certain and darted from his post to the bell, pulling the clacker hard and fast with three short strikes and then placing his hands on the bell's rim to quit the ring.

The men on deck scurried to their feet and made way to their posts. Lights went out across the ship.

From the darkness, only inches away, the captain's voice startled Morgana, who was unaware of his silent approach. "There were only three men against us in the room the first time he told that story. Don't let Mr. Erikson tell you fish tales," the captain said.

"Captain, I didn't know you were there," Erikson said.

"Best you go below to your room, ma'am. We need to run silent while we pass the lighthouse at Fort Jackson."

"We are at Fort Jackson already?"

"I told you, the *Ponthieva* is the fastest ship."

"I will never doubt you again, Captain," she said.

The captain could feel the warm flush return to his face from her words as he watched Erikson escort her below deck. It was a something that had not stirred in him since youth. More than the women in port could surface, it was something inside. He pushed away the distraction and tried to focus again on the moment of passing Fort Jackson.

Looking out the port hole from the deck below, Morgana whispered, "It only looks like a speck from here."

"It's not much more than that," Erikson replied. "But it is a mighty speck. Any one of those cannons could stop us if were any closer. Worse, they would signal one of the twelve armed vessels in the area to come find us."

Morgana turned and sank into the soft cushion of the cotton sack near the port side. "Tell me more about Captain Durand. He seems like such an interesting man, a powerful man."

"I'm glad to hear you like him so much. He has been a good captain to me and a good friend in any fight."

"You've been in fights?" she asked.

"Many."

"Have you ever killed a man?"

"When called for," he said with some guard. "Why do you ask?"

"I don't know. It seems like a big strong man like you or Captain Durand with a life of adventure on the sea might have stories. I am a practical woman, Mr. Erikson. I will do what I must. You must be practical too."

Erikson's tone went cold. "It's something I have done out of need, never out of joy. You stay here, stay silent, and I'll let you know when we are safe."

Morgana pondered aloud, "I wonder if I will have the chance to kill a man on this expedition . . . to know what it's like to take a life . . ."

Before his exit, a flash of the familiar recognition knowing exactly what that feeling was took away his normally light spirit. "I hope you never have to know."

"Maybe I will be good at it," she said without a thought.

"Being good at a thing has nothing to do with it. Being able to live with a thing is everything."

───➤◆◄───

Morgana found her hot day at sea to be dull. There was little for her to do. Her father was too busy with the navigation of maps and the interpretation of documents. The crew was too well trained and behaved to do more than be polite as they passed by her on the deck. Some of the men were more likely to watch her and pass by her with more frequency than others, especially when they were in tight spaces and there might be more than the common graze from her bustle.

Out of sheer boredom on the deck, while sitting on her chair, Morgana made an overt movement that lifted her dress to adjust her shoe. The hemline went so high that it caught the attention of eight men and resulted in one named Jones losing his footing and slipping overboard.

In response to this, several men started to throw objects that floated after him, including half-empty barrels and rope. By the time it took for the ship to slow, turn, recover the man, and return to full speed on course, they had lost three hours' time. A trail of debris any seaman worth his salt could follow marked that spot well.

"I will not stay in my room the rest of this voyage," Morgana said, pouting to her father. "I am not a child. I am a vital part of this work."

The doctor drew a deep breath to calm his nerves and said, "You are, Morgana, and you need to start behaving that way. Your antics on deck this afternoon are why the captain has asked you to stay here. He warned you on boarding that you are in his charge—you cannot play these games with the heads of his men. Enough danger waits for us."

"I know, Father," she conceded. "You are right. I will apologize to the captain at dinner and to Mr. Jones for my bad behavior. Maybe Mr. Erikson could escort me to his cabin?"

"I don't think that would be wise, my dear."

"Then you will take me."

"I will, but you must understand I have no time for these antics. We need to stay the course. The fountain is so close at hand. A lifetime of work is so near."

"I know, Father. This is important. This is why we are here."

⊂⊃ 5 ⊂⊃

Whispers

Year 2053
Olivia age 25

"WELL, THIS MORGANA is real slippy!" Olivia said. "She ain't wrapped too tight."

"Morgana?"

"Who would want to eat a dolphin? Really. I suspect she is more trouble than she is worth."

"She is beautiful."

"She might be good looking on the outside, but believe me, the old adage is true: it's what's inside that counts. I have had to learn that lesson more than once in my life."

"Troubles?"

"My former was nothing but trouble. When we first met, he was the sweetest. He thought of me first, paid special attention to me, but over time, that faded away. He had rough edges that I thought would soften, but they never did." Olivia reached into her bag and pulled out her mobile. The few pictures she kept were the reminders of why she could not answer his calls—the stiches across the right cheek, the black eye, the gash of torn skin on her neck where his class ring dug on a missed punch.

She talked to the man in the bed more to fill the silence than to explain, but he seemed to listen. "I used to blame myself. I thought that it was something I had done. He had convinced me of that. When the days were good, they were so good. It was as if the warm sun were shining on me alone and it would last all summer long. But then came the fall. And the first time, I thought it was me. The second, well." She sighed. "That third time, I knew it wasn't me. It was him. And I had to press charges, get the restraining order, move away."

"Where is home?" he asked.

"Wherever I carry it with me."

"I have seen things, been places," he said slowly. "I cannot remember them all, but I know I have been there, know that I have had a life of adventure."

"How old are you?"

"Old."

"Regrets?"

"Being good at a thing has nothing to do with it. Being able to live with a thing is everything," he quoted the book.

"You have read this book before?"

"I know it intimately. Please continue. You have such a lovely reading voice."

Chapter Three: Laguna de Términos

Year 1839
Viktor age 20
Morgana age 17

THE HEAT OF the fifth morning was unrelenting. Nothing Morgana did could avoid it, so she decided it would be best to change into her expedition outfit from the time she spent in Africa with her father. The pants were nothing a lady of the South would be seen in, but they were cool and comfortable, allowing her to be active. She discovered her father had done the same, selecting breathable fabrics to wear, when she met him for breakfast.

The men of the ship purposely distracted themselves with other activities in her presence to avoid temptation and falling over the rails. A slight nod was made when eyes connected at best. No one started a conversation with her. They were quick to step aside when she walked the decks. Her father, the captain, and Erikson were the only people she had any real interaction with, and that Erikson seemed a pleasant scoundrel with those blue eyes of his.

At the site of land, a flutter of activity filled the ship. St. Clair began to oversee the storage of items while Turner and a team opened the hatches, allowing for the retrieval of goods from below to be hoisted from the mainsail wrench.

Beautiful azure waters calmly lay ahead of the white sands that lined Laguna de Términos. Dolphins swam alongside the *Ponthieva*, guiding her into the lush waters full of life. Under the steady eye of the captain, Han was able to bring the *Ponthieva* to a river outlet close to land and drop the anchor.

Four small crafts were moved over the side of the boat and filled with the goods of the expedition. St. Clair was provided instructions along with the men who would stay behind. If there were no word from the landing party in six days, they were to send a small party after them to investigate. If another ship were to challenge them, they would run north to the city of Campeche and anchor beneath the fortified walls and cannon, requesting safe harbor.

Durand led the group in the first craft with the doctor, Erikson and Morgana were in the second with gear and crew, Turner was in charge of the third, and Han oversaw the last boat. The small chain went up stream through the winding waters lined with thick green canopies of tress throughout the afternoon. As the sun got closer to the top of the tree line, Durand signaled to land the crafts at a clearing.

They made camp on the shore. There was little relief from the heat in the darkness as it began to creep. Morgana found herself inching closer to the fire. When strange noises began to call from the unknown, she found herself next to Erikson.

"Enjoying the gloaming?" he asked.

"Not much," she replied. She knew well that he was teasing, but she couldn't enjoy his humor in the moment.

"There is nothing to worry about here. Look." He pointed across the river to the other bank where the soft lights of a million bugs began to glow in a pulse. "You won't see that in Georgia."

"Why, those are just lightning bugs and fireflies. We have those back home," she said.

"Not like that, not that many. Each is bigger than my fist, and that glow is not to light the way or scare off a predator, it's a mating call, the call of love."

"It is rather lovely. The soft glow is almost angelic, capturing little bits of heaven here on earth." She looked to him and caught those blue eyes looking at her again in the fire light. "Mr. Erikson, what is your Christian name?"

"It's Viktor, Viktor Erikson from Umeå, Sweden."

She smiled hearing his native accent more pronounced with certain words. "Viktor—that's a nice name. It means 'success' or 'winner' in English."

"Winning takes care of itself when you risk everything. What are you willing to risk?" he asked.

Morgana blushed from the attention. "If I needed a man, Mr. Erikson, I would have been married off years ago."

"There is need, and then there is want," he replied.

"I am nearly twenty years old, Mr. Erikson. I can do for myself."

He chuckled. "Shame."

"What is a shame?"

"Here we are, two fine human specimens, roughly the same age, beautiful, desired by others, and you tell me you can *do* for yourself."

"If I had stayed home instead of traveling with my father, most would think I am like old milk, past my prime. Yet I have done more and seen more than most back home will in a lifetime. I have traveled to four continents, ridden a camel, seen the pyramids at Giza, met lords and ladies in Europe, explored South America—I am far from expired. Life is too wonderful to waste raising babies and being pawed at by a scallywag every night. There is more to do than marry a man and watch him bully the workers on his plantation."

Erikson laughed.

"And what is so funny to you?"

"You are a most intelligent and experienced woman."

"And why is that funny?"

"I don't think I have ever met a woman like you before."

She felt a chill on her back. His blue eyes seemed to penetrate her soul and see her for who she truly was.

Softly, he repeated the words from a few nights before, "Certain women have a way of changing boys into men and some men back into boys."

"What do you mean?"

"You just reminded me of an admiral's daughter I once knew, that's all."

She didn't know just what to say to that, so she replied, "I will be turning in then, thank you." She made her way to the tent and tied the flap closed.

<hr/>

In the morning, before the full light of day cleared the canopy of the jungle, the expedition was packed and settled into the small crafts heading up the river again. When the boats came to narrows, the oars were used to push along the banks. When it was wide enough again, the men would row. Along the winding banks, there were birds and animals watching as the small vessels made their way up the slowing currents. The only sounds were the small splashes of paddles or the occasional instruction from Durand.

Past midday, the crafts beached and the men began to assemble the buckboard piled high with the parts for the sleds. A group removed large, sharp cutlasses from leather sheaths and started to hack at the greens, cutting a trail four men wide into the unknown. They followed what seemed to be a small path, only making it wider for the buckboard to follow. The pace was rather brisk as the team cutting would rotate after a few minutes with the men pushing the cart so that no man was too tired to stop momentum. Morgana followed with Turner near the rear while her father and Han stayed close to the front.

Another night of camping and a full day of forward movement followed before they reached an opening in the jungle that seemed to appear before them. The rise in the ground led to a foliage-covered stone structure. It was similar to the pyramids of Egypt but smaller. These were gray and the others golden. Both seemed ancient. It came with an audible relief from the men. The toll of pushing and cutting was high. It was difficult work, and they were happy to stop.

"This is it," the doctor said. "We should start here, but be careful. Do not move quickly here. We don't know what may lie in wait for us."

"Traps? Savages?" the captain said.

"These are guarded secrets. The people who built these temples would want to guard them from grave robbers and thieves. Be cautious of trip wires, falling rocks, and sharp hidden sticks. They will be difficult to see."

"You heard the doctor: be cautious of everything."

A new energy was found in the men. A team was assigned to work with Turner on the sleds, a smaller group went with Han, and the captain, Erikson, and the doctor joined Morgana in the exploration of the area.

There was more to the grounds than first appeared. They spent the day discovering piles of rocks that were once building and homes hidden by thick jungle. Trees growing straight up to daylight had split rocks, moved boulders, and divided these homes over the centuries. The remains of an ancient culture lay at their feet. For each decade of decay, it may well take another to uncover and identify the importance of this site.

Making a full survey of the surrounding area, they were able to identify and mark several of the dangerous traps that waited for the unsuspecting eye.

Finally, they made their way up the temple at the center of the site. Each of the main blocks of the temple was slightly higher than Erikson's waist. There was no quick way to climb until a series of steps was found. There were hundreds, if not thousands, of worn gray stones, several loose, giving way under the weight of the team traversing to the top.

It was a glorious view at this elevation, worth the hard work of getting there. One could see just above the tree line. Just as rewarding was the chamber entrance they discovered. A small assembly of stones in a certain way allowed for an entrance. Bird, bats, guano, and general dirt buildup over the centuries covered the main corridor. It looked unpleasant to walk through. Erikson held the team back from entering and drew his sidearm. A single shot into the darkness of the temple sent a shocking burst of the flying mammals to flight. The rush of wings through the air felt like a stiff breeze at the bow of the *Ponthieva* during a headwind. After the last of the dark animals fled the chamber, Erikson gave the signal to move forward with the lantern.

∽ 7 ∾

Chapter Four: The Pyramid

Year 1839
Viktor age 20
Morgana age 17

"**G**OLD," ERIKSON SAID. "Pure gold has no tarnish. This is dust and dirt." He wiped away the grime from the article on the wall. Han drew the lantern closer, revealing its natural gleam.

"I bet these haven't seen the light of day in centuries," the captain added.

"Mr. Erikson, please." The doctor stopped him. "Do not remove it from the wall yet."

Erikson stepped back and complied.

"There are more on the walls. Look"—the doctor pointed—"it's a map."

"We need to clean these, not remove them," Morgana said.

With a nod, Erikson understood and began to clean them with his handkerchief. Han and the captain removed their own handkerchiefs to do the same. As they finished one piece of ornamental gold on the wall, another next to it was discovered. The more they cleaned, the more they understood about this mosaic map on the wall.

After an hour of brushing away grime from the centuries, they stood back to appreciate the work.

"One hundred and thirty-six by my count," Erikson said about the items, small and large, on the wall before them.

"That is a treasure, my friends," the captain said.

"This is our map to the fountain," the doctor replied. "Look here." He pointed. "The markings—this is the pyramid we are in, and this is the one next to it across the field."

"So, there are more? All of them may have gold in them," Erikson said.

"Not all of them," the doctor explained. "See how this one is shaped? It's different than that, these markings." He pointed to the gold on the wall. "Different than these. I believe that this would be the only one with a map of gold. The other was a place of sacrifice and worship."

"Sacrifice?" Han asked.

"These people were quick to give their lives to their gods. Beheading and slaying humans, not animals, were their gifts to the heavens."

"Where is your fountain, Doctor? We've found our gold," the captain said.

"I will need time to study this. Morgana and I will copy the map from the wall and decipher it. Once we are done, you can take your treasure."

"Mr. Han, Mr. Erikson, not a word of this yet to the men. We don't want anyone to get ideas of their own out here. I'll tell Mr. Turner so he can decide how we are going to carry this down, load the buckboard and sleds, and get it back to the ship."

"Aye," the two replied to his command.

"Doctor, what will you need from us?"

"Another lamp, some water, a little food maybe."

Han left the chamber, getting the nod from the captain.

"Mr. Erikson, you have the first watch here. We are going to need to find a way to keep our flying friends from coming back home to roost."

"Aye."

Atop the ancient structure, the de la Mottes tried to sleep on the exterior stone. Erikson sat with his back against the block, looking over the foliage to the distance through his glass.

"Can't sleep," Morgana told him, sitting next to him. "How do you do it?"

"When a man gets tired enough, nothing can shake him up," he replied.

She leaned her head on his arm, seeking some comfort of sleep. He didn't mind. "I thought a hard man like you might be softer than the rock," she said.

"I'm not a hard man. Durand is a hard man. He tells me I am the only man to ever make him smile, and I am not that funny."

"What will you do with your share?" she asked.

"It will start with hot bath. I will add a clean shave. A bottle of whiskey next."

"A woman?"

"Any woman? Or a certain woman?"

"A certain woman could be there."

"Well, there she is in the hot bath next to me and enjoying my whiskey. What a nice dream."

"I would buy some land. A nice place I could call my own. I don't want to need for anything."

"That, too, is a nice dream."

"Dream? I can do that," she said.

"More than likely, my life won't change. I enjoy a life at sea. These jungles, the cities, they are only a place to visit."

"Have you been to Alaska?"

"I have."

"I've always wanted to go. Have you ever faced the Ottomans?"

"Ha! What kind of question is that?"

"I hear they are fierce fighters, brave, and courageous."

"Men are men wherever I go. They want one of three things: a beautiful woman, good drink, or a good time, and they don't have to be in that order."

"I wish life were that simple for me. The men I know tell me what to do, where to go, and how to act. I would like to do what I want, find some mischief, see what adventures there are out there."

"Well, there you have it, Morgana. You won't find that on your own plot of land. You need to sail the world with me."

"You are not that hard of a man. Not hard to understand." She closed her eyes and found all the rest she could that night.

A gunshot rang out, waking everyone in camp and on the pyramid. It was first light after a long night. The sound sent the few dark mammals to flight that had tried to return before sunrise. The doctor and his daughter returned to their work.

Erikson gave a wave to the ground for "all clear."

"Mr. Turner, what plans have you for us?" Durand asked.

"Depends on our timing, Captain," he replied. "Best way to carry this is to melt it down into bars. We can stack them even on the buckboard and roll out of here, leaving the sleds behind. But that takes some time. Two days, maybe."

"The fast way?" the captain said.

"We put each in a sack and strap it down. But with all that moving around, we are going to need to stop and tighten up the lines to make sure we don't lose any."

"We need to get word to the *Ponthieva* of our plans if we are going to take longer. Dr. de la Motte needs to be done quick. I don't want to be caught in this jungle by surprise."

"What are you going to need to melt down the gold?" Erikson asked Turner.

"Yesterday scouting around, we found some brick kilns on the far side of the other pyramid. We might be able to get those hot enough."

The captain said, "Take three men and see what you can do to make molds for us. If you can melt it down all the way, maybe we can make it easier to carry. Heading down stream should help make for a quick return."

"Aye," Turner replied, pointing to three men to join him.

Going up and down the pyramid became tiresome, so Durand waved Erikson to meet him half way. "How is progress?"

"They seem to be done with the map. They are trying to translate what it means now."

"I don't want them up there another night. I want to get that gold down and be on our way quick-like."

"Aye. Most of the work got done last night. Better done quick than wait another night. Would not want to be foolish like that time we had to drop our cargo on Ossabaw Island. We buried some fine friends there," Erikson said.

"And some fine enemies too."

"We got out alive."

"Yes, but who else cares? Who else even remembers?" Durand pondered.

"Captain." The doctor beckoned him from above. "Captain."

The two men made their way up the stone steps.

"I've translated what I need, so you can start to get your men," he explained. "You can take the gold now." The doctor unfolded the large flap of thick paper. "Here is where we are," he said, setting it on the stone for the others. "This is our pyramid. Over there is the fountain and next to it another pyramid. I suspect that will have more gold in it."

"And these others?" the captain asked.

Han came up the steps quickly behind them.

"No, those were temples for prayer, like the one over there." He pointed across the field.

"Mr. Han, where do you think that mark on the map is?"

Catching his breath, Han removed a flap of paper and unfolded it to reveal a larger map of the area. He looked between the two carefully. "Captain, that is two days from here in that direction." He pointed east. "It is the base of this mountain range here." He pointed back to the larger map.

Durand sat on the nearest step and looked east to the mountains. Near the base of the other pyramid, he could see Turner working on the kilns. In the camp, the rest of the crew waited for instruction.

"Two days, Mr. Han?"

"Each way."

The captain contemplated the options, readjusted his hat to sit on his head just right, and looked to Erikson.

"What's on your mind, Captain?"

"Mr. Erikson, have the crew start to remove the gold from the map room, take it over to Mr. Turner, and have him do his best to melt them into bars. Ask Mr. Rico to return to the *Ponthieva* with this message if they are still there: ten days."

"Ten days, Captain?"

"He will wait ten days. You, the good doctor, his daughter, Mr. Han, and I will go find the fountain while Mr. Turner and the crew are to melt the gold and return it to the *Ponthieva*. He will need to leave one of the skiffs for us on the river. We will be moving fast."

"Aye, Captain."

❦ 8 ❦

Awkward

Year 2053
Olivia age 25

"**O**LIVIA?" THE QUESTION came from the door.
"Yes, I am Olivia."
Her hand reached out to shake. "I thought I saw your name on the roster tonight. I'm Claytie Tulin, head nurse, one of the team considering your application. I had gotten word you were volunteering in the NODA ward."

"Yes, it is good to meet you. I enjoy volunteering."

"It's great to see this kind of spirit in an applicant."

"Being a part of *this* team is something I view as being very special, so I am happy to help in any way I can."

"Thank you, that is very encouraging," Claytie said. "Who are you with this evening?"

"This patient came in as a John Doe, but he told me his name is Viktor Erikson. That's also the name inscribed in the book he arrived with. He also keeps asking for a woman named Morgana," Olivia explained.

"Viktor Erikson?" Claytie pondered. "That name seems so familiar to me. We have an Erikson on our board. How is Viktor spelled?"

"With a *K*, not a *C*."

"Yeah, the same way. Kind of an odd way to spell Viktor."

Olivia held up the book to Claytie. "You can see."

"I'll have to check. Maybe it's the same one. His house—and by 'house' I mean 'estate,' all these houses are on huge estates around here—is nearby. Only minutes away. I'll ask around."

"That would be great. I know that the detective investigating the hit-and-run that brought him here was going to try and track him down as well," Olivia explained.

"Well, it was good to see you. Thank you for sitting with Viktor. I hope we get the chance to see each other again during the interview process," Claytie said. She shook hands again.

"I look forward to that," Olivia said.

The beeping noise from Claytie's communication collar started to beep. A tap to the device activated it, allowing her to talk. "Claytie Tulin, how can I help you?" She smiled politely and exited the door in conversation.

Olivia was left alone again, accompanied only by the pulsing beeps and whirs of the machines reporting Viktor's condition. "It would be an interesting coincidence to find that you are the same Viktor Erikson in this bed was the as the one on the board of directors for the hospital," she said aloud. Then, she considered it would be even more amazing if this Viktor were related to the one in this story. Perhaps he was the great-grandson of the Viktor in the book, a name passed down to each generation. The book seemed substantial enough to be a reflection based on the family heritage.

After using the bathroom, Olivia contemplated her appearance in the mirror. She wore the scrubs from the last hospital that were traditional teal. She noticed that the ones Claytie wore were purple. Other nurses had blue, some orange, the doctors wore navy, and the staff in the children's ward had yellow duckies. She wasn't sure if the colors indicated a department or a role, but it would be a question to ask during her next interview.

Olivia once loved her hair. As a girl, it was long and golden, very Germanic, like all of her sisters and brothers. A trip to the hairdresser would do her wonders. It may be necessary to find additional dollars in her budget before the next interview. In two months' time, she would be through her savings and have move past needing this job to being desperate for any job.

Today, at this late hour, with oily skin, greasy hair, little makeup, and wearing old scrubs, she was certainly comfortable but not at her best presentation-wise. It was both positive and unfortunate to see Claytie in this state. What should have been clear was her dedication to the hospital.

The little tune on her phone from her former jingled again. There had been moments when that tune would bring a smile to her face, when she knew he was thinking of her and they would be together again. Now that little ditty only brought a flash of annoyance that he would not stop thinking about her, that he was seeking her out in a moment of weakness. Her mind would return to that moment when she opened her eyes to find him above her with clenched fists, tears in his eyes, and his regrettable repetition of the phase "Why did you make me do that? You shouldn't have made me do that."

Once she found the phone in her bag, she set it to mute. Repeatedly thinking of a topic, dwelling on that instant, would reinforce the neurons and firing of synapses in the brain. Thinking about one thing too much would lead to the strengthening of that thought. She wanted him out of her life. She had to stop thinking about it to make certain she would stop thinking of him in the future.

With phone in hand, she did a quick search for Laguna de Términos—a real location—and the pinch and swipe of her fingers showed the blue waters described, a river large enough to journey against the flow into the deep jungle. With only a quick scan for pyramids in the area, she found a few. She learned that the Maya civilization, once large and powerful, disappeared upon the arrival of conquistadors from Spain. The details were still not known after centuries of research. They were either killed in huge numbers, died from the lack of antibodies to defend against the Europeans, or escaped by blending into the surrounding cultures and never returned.

"Water," Viktor whispered.

Olivia returned to her chair at his side and held the cup closer to his mouth, inserting the straw and watching him draw. When he finished, she set the cup back on the tray by his bed.

Between sips, he completed the sentence, "It's hard to imagine . . . the courage it takes . . . to care for others."

"It is not that difficult for me; I was raised a certain way," she said.

His face changed to an expression of curiosity.

She explained, "I was raised to care for others, mostly my siblings—we had a big family."

"I can't remember," he said.

"You can't remember?"

"The *Ponthieva*, I can't remember her."

"What do you remember?"

"Morgana."

"You know what helps me to think and focus? A game. Let's play a little game. What do you find awkward but really shouldn't?"

His head turned to her, his eye open as if this were something wonderful to take his mind off the moment.

"I'll go first," she said with a warm smile. "I find it awkward to open presents in front of other people when they don't have presents, but I shouldn't feel that way."

Viktor smiled for the first time in front of Olivia. Even though it was quick, she caught it. His voice was still a wisp as he said, "I find it awkward when people sing 'Happy Birthday.' I am happy when they remember, but it is odd to have people sing to you."

She giggled. "That is awkward. I find it awkward when I say 'goodbye' on the phone or 'bye-bye' or 'so long.' I feel like we should just end the call faster."

"I find it awkward to use public toilets," he said.

"That is awkward. I find it awkward to say 'thanks, you too' when I'm at a retail store."

"Buying condoms or sanitary napkins should not be awkward, yet it is."

"Viktor!" Olivia proclaimed. "You are so right."

He began to cough in the excitement, and she provided him more water. After recovering, he said, "I find it awkward that a total stranger can be easier to talk to than a person you have known for a lifetime."

"Viktor, you can tell me anything you want. We are both human, and I am happy to listen," Olivia assured him.

"I can't remember my past, Olivia."

"You did hit your head, Viktor. You may start to remember again. It might just take time."

"Maybe," he gasped.

"Would you like me to keep reading?"

His voice was weak and raspy. "Yes, please read."

Olivia opened the book to find razor-cut edges of a few chapters. "There are some pages missing here."

"It skips in part. I can't remember why—how awkward."

She giggled at his wit. "Well, they look cut, intentional."

"Morgana may have removed the pages. She is always trying to protect me from the past or from myself."

"I don't understand why she would do that."

His face was innocent and clear looking up to her.

"There must have been some bad parts here?" she asked.

His good hand pulled up the cover to his neck. "Please keep reading."

Chapter Seven: Return to Laguna de Términos

Year 1839
Viktor age 20
Morgana age 17

THE SHOT'S SHARP crack echoed, grabbing the attention of every man on the *Ponthieva*'sz deck. St. Clair and Rico watched as the skiff took speed from the river's momentum, shooting into the calm, safe harbor waters of Laguna de Términos. Natives chased the skiff from the jungle to the white sands of the beach, stopping only when the bravest were waist-deep.

"Mr. Rico, to arms," St. Clair commanded.

Rico shouted orders of his own and was able to produce a swivel gun to the deck, ready for a shot in less than a minute.

"Fire a warning shot away from the skiff," St. Clair said.

After ignition, a thunderous crack followed a plume of smoke, sending a fountain of water near the natives. The noise and demonstration sent them back to the jungle in confusion.

All hands were called to help the skiff's passengers board.

"Mr. Erikson, Ms. de la Motte, welcome aboard," St. Clair said. "Where is the captain? Mr. Han? The doctor?"

The crew passed a bundle up from the skiff followed by a second in a bucket line until both were safely in the hands of Morgana.

"It is difficult to explain, Mr. St. Clair," Viktor replied.

Looking closer at these two bundles, St. Clair could see that they were babies: one Caucasian, the other Asian.

Looking in disbelief, St. Clair asked, "And your father?"

Viktor looked to Morgana and said with a touch of sadness, "Didn't make it."

"The savages?" St. Clair asked.

Viktor thought before answering. "I will tell you all the full tale once we are safely underway." Turning to Morgana, he said, "Why don't you take them to the captain's quarters and clean up? Mr. St. Clair, raise anchor and make best speed to New Orleans."

"New Orleans, sir?"

"In light of our current state, Mr. St. Clair, I'll take command of the *Ponthieva*, moving you from third to second. New Orleans is the nearest commercial safe harbor. We walked right into a skirmish between republicans and *federales*, and they drove us right into the natives a day back. We have been on the run for days and could use rest."

"Aye," St. Clair said. He then passed on the orders to get underway.

Before leaving the deck, Viktor turned back. "By the way, Mr. St. Clair, did Mr. Turner and the crew return with the gold?"

"Aye, sir. They brought back polished bricks, sir."

"Very good. I'll be in the captain's quarters."

He walked down the rickety steps to the cooler air of the lower deck. Behind the sliding door, Morgana was setting down the babies, now pinned with fresh clothes around their bottoms, onto the captain's bedding. She looked at them. They looked back at her. Viktor's entrance took all of their attention.

Morgana stepped to Viktor and let him hold her. She felt safe there. "Viktor" was all she could let out.

Gently, he lifted her head with a curled finger. When their eyes met, he leaned in and kissed her, long and deep. He breathed her in, filling his sense with her.

"So much has happened in such a short time," she whispered.

"I know, but we are safe. *You* are safe here."

"The babies don't cry or fuss. They just look at me, as if they know what has happened to them . . . they're just unable to speak."

"We don't know what the effects will be or how long they will last. We just have to be patient."

"Did they bring back the gold?" she asked.

"Mr. St. Clair informs me they were able to melt it into bars for safe transfer to the ship."

"Where will we go? What will we do?"

"We are heading to New Orleans. Over the next few days, avoiding any trouble, we should be in a safe port."

"There will be questions, many questions."

"I know. We will have to tell them," he said.

"Everything?"

"Well, nearly everything. The men deserve to know what happened to their captain, to Mr. Han." He took the bag off his shoulder and removed the three silver flasks, one marked with an *X*, setting them on the table. "They look harmless sitting there full like that."

"Why don't you clean up? I can look after these two," she said.

"I will once these are locked up." He took the three flasks, placed them in the captain's safe, and locked them away quickly.

"Tell me, Mr. Turner, any trouble once we left?" Viktor asked.

"No, sir." Turner explained, "I was able to get the kilns hot enough to melt the gold. We dropped the molten gold into wet clay molds and shaped them into bars. Once they cooled, we broke open the molds, polished them up, and loaded them into these crates. It was fairly easy to move them as bars with just the one buckboard."

"And you were careful to get all the gold?"

"Yes, sir, every speck. There is more gold in your teeth than was left behind that day."

"Very good. Let's see how it turned out," Viktor said. He watched Turner remove the key from the leather strap around his neck and open each of the four large cases.

"They were heavy, Mr. Erikson. Each of these took four men to carry by hand to the skiffs once they got off the buckboard. We found some shallow spots on that river heading back too."

The gold seemed to glow in an unnatural light. Each bar was beautiful. They glistened and dazzled the eyes of Viktor as he looked in. "It looks so different here than on those dirty walls of that pyramid."

"They do," Turner said.

"It's captivating."

"They are—I had better close them up, just to be safe."

"Of course. Thank you, Mr. Turner."

"What happened out there? What happened to the captain? Mr. Han?" Turner asked.

"It is a difficult tale." Viktor looked to the door and spoke low and close, "We found the fountain."

Turner's eyes grew large. "It was there?"

"It was horrifying. The water had this magic. It transformed the men after drinking it. The screams were . . ." He fell silent in the memory. "There were two fountains. The doctor couldn't decipher all the text, and so—"

"Viktor," Morgana called in a stern voice from the top of the steps, "may I have words with you?"

———⫸⧫⫷———

The lovers, together in each other's arms again, enjoyed more than pillow talk in the captain's quarters.

"I've been thinking, Viktor."

"Thinking about what?"

"Why New Orleans? Why not back to Savannah? Why not to Havana? We have a fast ship that can go anywhere in the world. Why there?"

"What about the men? We owe them their split of the gold. We owe Captain Durand and Mr. Han a doctor. Don't we?"

"They knew what they were doing, especially the captain once Mr. Han drank the water," she said.

"We didn't know what it would do."

"He was there. You were there. The screams of pain, the sounds of anguish—I will never be able to clear those from my mind. But he drank it anyway, just a little, and he followed Mr. Han in his return to infancy."

"I wonder what it's like. Do you think they know?" he pondered.

"They are babies. What do they know?"

"Still, they are not like any babies I have known."

"How many babies have you spent time with?"

"Not many . . . my brothers when they were young."

"They are like any other babies I have seen. Babies," she huffed. "I thought my adventures would take me away from them, but here I am with two." She was silent for a while in thought. "Viktor, we could take the babies to an orphanage. That way, we wouldn't need to raise them."

"What? No. That's Captain Durand and Mr. Han!"

"Is it? Is it really? They are babies, Viktor, not the men you once knew and respected."

"What if they snap out of it? What if the effects can be reversed?" he pleaded.

"What if they can't?" she said. "They will have full lives ahead of them. They get to have another full life, set off the worries of old age, delay death, live for a brighter future."

"Avoid the mistakes."

"Yes. If I could have a second chance, believe me, there are many things I would do differently," she said.

"Like what?"

"I would pack better for these expeditions, for one," she said, getting up. "I would care less for what others say about me or try to impose on me. I would be more independent."

"You are already the most independent woman I know."

"I would do more. I have proven time and again that I am just as smart as any man. I am just as brave as you."

"And more."

"So why shouldn't I get to try for a better life? One that is mine?"

"Do you want to be a baby again?"

"No," she said honestly, "not especially." She stepped away from the bed and put her nightgown back on.

He could see her shape and beauty outlined by the moonlight through the sheer gown. The time with her made him crave more of her flesh, entangle with her body, kiss her skin, and smell her sweetness.

"What is on your mind, Viktor?"

"Besides you?"

"Yes."

"How to divide all that gold among the men. Once we pay some men, they'll leave. This is a good crew. I would hate to lose them. All the same, once we go to port and the stories get out about how much gold we carry, we'll become a target. Every pirate, swindler, and cheat will want a part of the ship and this crew. Port fees will go up when they find what we have." He sighed at the thought and responsibility it carried. "Everyone wants their cut."

"This crew, this ship, needs a leader. They need someone to fill that void where the strong hand of Captain Durand once held them in line. You need to be that leader."

"Go on."

"You are next in command; you are the next logical choice."

"I am."

"This is your crew now. These are your men, your ship. Where are you going to lead them?"

"New Orleans."

"Where some will leave you once they have the gold. Word will spread. You will be a target. Those who remain on the *Ponthieva* will be a target."

"You are right."

"Thieves, scoundrels, and scalawags will hear about the *Ponthieva* and what she carries, about all the riches on one ship, and come after her. You will always be on the run."

Her words began to make sense to him like the serpent in Eden.

"This is your one opportunity to make things right," she said. "You don't want to have to kill more men in defense of this treasure that is rightfully yours."

"I don't want to have to kill or hurt anyone again."

"So, we have to think of a way to prevent harm to this crew, *your* crew. Think of a way that we can keep them from leaving to tell others about this gold."

It came to him. "The water?"

"The water," she confirmed. "We could take the water of life and place it in the cantina during a meal." Morgana returned to the bed. She began to kiss him in the places he liked in the way he liked, slowly moving the strap from her shoulder again to reveal more of her skin. "What if there were a way to keep all the gold, keep the men safe, and keep the ship from harm? As captain, wouldn't it be your duty to take that action?"

"It sounds bad."

She kissed him again, this time on the lips. "There is no bad, no good. The point to life is to be more developed, more fruitful. How will these men ever find a good drink, a good woman, or a good time if they are being hunted by criminals for gold? You need to protect them."

The *Ponthieva* set anchor in the darkness off the port of New Orleans to a small berth. Mountains of baled cotton filled the docks, ready for loading on the line of steam ships and paddleboats. So busy were workers that the small but speedy ship went unnoticed. A single soul leapt from the deck of the *Ponthieva* and landed on the dock. He set the plank and then walked a block to hire a buckboard and a man to help.

The two men proceeded to load the buckboard with twenty-nine bundles of freshly wrapped babies. He explained to the driver that they were poor orphans from a mission and needed a good Christian upbringing. The driver, the man, and the twenty-nine babies traveled the New Orleans streets to the clip-clop rhythm of the horses' hoofs until they reached the French Mission. The nuns of the church took the children under their care along with two gold bars. On safe return to the *Ponthieva*, the driver received a generous bag of coins for his late hour's work.

Silently, the ship slipped back into the darkness of the Mississippi river, sailing with the current into the Gulf.

Chapter Eight: Fort Brooke

Year 1839
Viktor age 20
Morgana age 17

"WHAT DO WE do now?" Morgana asked.

Viktor didn't answer. He was still shaken from the events of the previous day. Even locked away in the captain's room while the crew had eaten their meal, he could hear the initial screams turn into confusion, the madness of not knowing what was happening to their own bodies morph. The transformation of the adult male writhing in pain to the high-pitched wails of an infant's call repeated itself in the ship's galley for a solid quarter of an hour and then subsided.

"Viktor?" she called. "Viktor, are you with me?"

He ignored her calls and instead rose, walked down the stairs to the galley, removed the two water vessels the the men drank from that previous day, and proceeded to carry them up the steps, throwing them over the side. With a sense of accomplishment in having done the deed, he said, "I am with you."

She looked a little frightened by his rage. She had heard the word "berserker" in regard to the Nordic men when they fall into a trance-like state of fury to fight. She thought this might be a glimpse into his outer limits when pushed. "All right, good, you are with me," she calmly said. "What do we do next? We need to have a plan or think about the best next actions. We cannot sit anchored here off the coast forever. We are eventually going to need to make port."

Viktor sat on the step leading up to the wheel. Head in hand, his first attempts to focus were struggled. "We will need to find a crew," he muttered. "No, a small crew, five men, no more than ten. I will not be able to get far with just you and me."

"Yes," she encouraged the progress. "Five to ten men who can sail. Five to ten men who can sail that we can trust. Where can we find such men?"

"Who can we trust?"

The two sat listening to the waves lap against the hull of the ship. The one question was of trust. They only had one another. They had to trust one another to live.

"I trusted the men we abandoned in New Orleans," he said.

"We have gone over this. We had to do that for their own good, to protect them from the fever that comes with all that gold. None of them would have been safe."

"And now we bare that sickness alone."

By day's end, the two had managed to bring up the anchor and set sail at a slow but manageable speed east. In what normally would have taken the *Ponthieva* two days' time, they were able to reach Fort Brooke in four days under a friendly flag.

The weathered brown-gray walls of Fort Brooke did not look welcoming. Rowing to shore in the skiff, the two could see the watchful eyes from the shore. The soldiers standing guard with musket barrels peeking over the earthen berm looked like reeds all in a row sticking over the top. Stories had circled about the struggles these men had withstood from Seminole attack.

Morgana's smile seemed to lighten the hearts of men when they landed. Her beauty was the key. Viktor knew he would not have been able to do this alone. This was abundantly clear when they were introduced to the general in command.

"General Zachary Taylor," he introduced himself, taking her hand. "What an unexpected pleasure to meet you, Ms. de la Motte."

"You are so kind, General." Her Southern lilt came on strong. "It is a pleasure to meet you as well."

"My men inform me you survived an attack of some sort?" he asked.

"Oh, it was horrible, General. We had anchored about a day north, and the landing party went out and never returned. Dear Mr. Erikson was left behind to watch over me and the ship while my father, the good Dr. de la Motte, whom I am sure you have heard of, went on looking for new and abnormal flora."

The rugged general turned to Viktor. "I assume you are Mr. Erikson?"

"Yes, General."

"And you were able to sail the ship and Ms. de la Motte safely here?"

"Please, General," she interrupted, "do call me Morgana. You have been so kind to meet with us. You should call me by my first name."

"Thank you, Morgana. You were able to bring her here to safety, Mr. Erikson?"

"Yes, General," Viktor answered.

"And your crew, how long have they been missing?"

"They were to give word in five days, and it has been ten."

The general tried to force an expression of comfort on his gruff face but only achieved the slight curl of his right lip. He placed his hand on Morgana's arm and explained, "My dear girl, I fear the worst may have happened to your father and the crew. You see, we are in the midst of a fierce battle. I would like to show you something, if I may?"

"Yes, please."

He guided Morgana to the window in his office overlooking the parade ground inside the fort. "What do you know about dogs, Morgana?"

"Oh, I adore them." She said with a sugary Southern emphasis, "Just love dogs."

"Those dogs are a breed called bloodhound. They have been bred to be the best hunting dogs that have set four paws on this great earth. They can smell and track down anything they put their mind to, and these are trained to hunt down these savage Seminoles."

"Oh my, hunting dogs chasing down a man?"

"These are not men. These are Indians. These are killers. If your father and the crew are still alive, these dogs will be able to find them and my men will bring them here." Retrieving an unlaundered shirt from the ship, the general sent fifty of his men north with the dogs to retrieve her father and make good on his promise.

Viktor took this opportunity to inquire in the surrounding camps about men who might be interested in helping him sail the *Ponthieva* north if the crew was not recovered. He was able to find seven such men, six of whom had experience at sea and one who would work for safe passage away from Seminole territory.

After fourteen days, thirty-two men and most of the dogs returned to report that they found and killed a large Indian party in the area described, but the crew and the doctor had not been recovered and were presumed dead or lost.

Her portrayal of grief was remarkable. It seemed very realistic. Viktor, watching the general comfort her in his arms, wondered if she had ever played him in the same way when seeing this performance. Morgana had told Viktor that the tales she told the general were only to establish the loss of her father and the crew, preventing any gossip in the social circle which filled Georgia. Her mind seemed to work on more levels than that of a simple sailor interested in gold and treasure. Morgana was able to turn her tongue, slip her sleeve to reveal a little shoulder, and win the trust of almost any man in the fort and surrounding camp with little effort. He just wanted enough competent men to board the ship and help him find a permanent crew.

With so many unanswered questions about the waters, Viktor considered the notion that he needed another person's mind on the matter. Someone like her father who knew science, but not one that could play him the fool.

———>•<———

With one arm on the wheel and the other wrapped around her waist, Viktor commanded the seven men north on the *Ponthieva* through the night. She stood between him and the wheel in rapture, plotting for the next day, no man within earshot of their voices.

"I have only known a life at sea. The ship and sail is my life," he explained.

"Viktor, how can you keep all this gold safe on a ship? We must pass dozens of other vessels each day. It would only take one with a larger crew, a bigger gun, and more will to take this all away from us. To take me from you."

"That is true, Morgana: there are many risks we face every day."

"So, the *wise* thing to do would be to have a home, a place to call our own, away from the prying eyes of others."

"You don't want to go home to Georgia? Find a nice home in Savanah?"

"Too many people know me in Georgia. They would ask about my father daily . . . so many questions about the house we would buy, the status we would hold."

"We could go to Boston. No one would know you there. We could find a bank to deposit the gold."

"Banks get robbed—we can't deposit in a bank. And Boston is too cold."

"New York?"

"That fire trap? The city nearly burned to the ground only a few years ago. How safe can that be?"

"So outside of Manhattan. Maybe somewhere along the Erie Canal for good commerce, a port to the sea."

"Oh, that would be nice! Something on the water for you, but a plantation for me."

The two would be lucky to reach the Atlantic as the new men on board were poor at best with their work. A small gale would send them a-scurrying, grabbing for ropes and in a sweat. Fortune was on the crew's side as they made port in Philadelphia, and the ship's manifest holding several large bills of tender allowed them to dock without inspection.

The seven men departed without word or incident being paid in full. Viktor went ashore to find five true sailors for hire to take them to New Haven. Finding five good men in the port of Philadelphia was not difficult. It took a matter of an hour to find a familiar face and recruit four more by reference. Viktor paid well, and the task was relatively easy.

In the remaining hours of daylight, before the tides on the Delaware turned out of favor, Viktor decided to seek advice on the grounds of the Perelman School of Medicine. After a few polite conversations, he was directed and introduced to Professor Leidy, who was sitting at a laboratory desk and peering into an eyepiece.

"Professor Leidy?"

"Yes." The bearded man looked up.

"My name is Viktor Erikson, captain of the *Ponthieva*."

Yellowish teeth were revealed as the dark hair parted like a stage curtain. "That is a good name for a ship. Do you transport flora?"

"At times, when the pay is right, we will ship nearly anything."

"How can I help you, Mr. Erikson?" Leidy asked.

"In my journeys, I have come across many wondrous things I cannot explain."

"I can imagine."

"In recent months, I have been witness to a substance that has transformed the way a man behaves, his very nature. I was curious if you have come along the same findings."

"Interesting, very interesting. I do know of foods and fauna that have changed behavior. By Merton's rules, these are mostly in the *Agaricales* genus." Leidy smiled. "Mushrooms."

"Yes, mushrooms would have that effect on behavior," Viktor said politely. "What about the change in a man's appearance? Are there such foods or plants that might change a man, to say, be younger, stronger, vital?"

The professor chuckled. "There are many elixirs available on the street corner with those claims but nothing with such lasting impact or potency, I know of."

Viktor sighed, unsure of how much he could discuss without seeming mad. "Is there—"

"Say it, man," Leidy interrupted. "Tell me what you witnessed. These persistent questions around the point bore me to no end, and I have better things to do with my time."

"I witnessed something that I cannot believe, that seems untrue, that is fantastic, that I cannot explain. A man drank a potion and turned into a baby—no trick, no illusion, no magic. In plain daylight, I watched his skin retract and bones shrink. The shrills and screams of pain were unbearable. Yet this substance he found, at some small level, included something powerful, something transformational."

Leidy look the man over. "I believe you saw something you may not understand. It is nothing I have ever known. You are suggesting there are powers that are so small they cannot be observed by the human eye."

"Yes, it was in this water."

"The water turned a man into a child."

"An infant."

"And there was something in this water, something you could not see, that was more potent than anything observed or documented?" Leidy said.

"It sounds ridiculous; I am sure of that. Yet I was witness to it on more than one occasion," Viktor explained. "I was hoping that it was not unimaginable."

With a deep breath, the professor adjusted himself in the chair. "Small and powerful forces at play in everyday items like water that could change or alter the state of a man." He turned to his desk and jotted down the idea. "Sir, I do not know what it was, but it is not unimaginable. I have yet to witness it myself. Do you have this substance, this water?"

"I do."

"If you were able to bring me a sample, if I were able to explore and understand it in my laboratory, I could give you a better answer."

"I understand. Thank you very much for your time, Professor Leidy. Thank you." Viktor turned and made his way to the door.

On return to the *Ponthieva*, he found himself under watchful eyes of Morgana.

"What took you so long?" she asked.

"I hired a team of men: one I had known, the others he trusted."

"That could not have taken you all day. There must have been something else."

"Just finding the right men."

"While I sat here alone on the ship. What if someone had come? What if someone had tried to force themselves on me? Find our treasure?"

Viktor asked, "Why are you so upset? Nothing happened to you, Morgana."

"I want to know the truth. What else were you up to? I need to trust you and you me; we are bound together in trust."

"I thought it might be something else."

"Something else? Like what?"

"Love."

"Oh yes, well, of course, that too. But what good will love do me if you are off drinking with the boys in the tavern while I am here alone?"

"Do you smell a drop on me? I hired men, I met a man on campus, we talked a little, and then I returned."

"Oh, now there is a trip to the university? What else did you fail to mention?"

"Morgana, I don't understand this. Why are you acting this way?"

"You just keep in mind that I know you, Viktor. I know what you have done, and I am watching you. Be careful of your step," she warned. "I need to trust you completely with the secrets we hold, the treasures we keep." With her rubbish cheeks filled with bluster, she stared to his discomfort until a splash of paddles in the water caught her attention: the team of hired men approached in a skiff. "I am always watching," she said.

Under her watchful eyes, there was no opportunity to take samples of the waters. Each time Viktor had tried to be alone and make his way to the captain's safe, she would discover him. She was full of questions about the city, about when they would set sail again. After bearing witness to what had transpired before New Orleans and her ability at such convincing deception with General Taylor, Viktor thought it best not to mention his curiosity with Professor Leidy.

When the men settled to the *Ponthieva*, his hope of connecting with the professor was gone. They would set sail for New Haven, find a plantation-size property, and build a fortress home to keep safe the treasure . . . where she would keep a watchful eye on his every activity. They would only trust each other.

⁓ 11 ⁓

Turn

Year 2053
Olivia age 25

"**S**HE LIED AND men died," Olivia said.
"*La pasión para sobrevivir* is what the Spanish call it: passion for survival."

"But it's not justifiable. How can she just get away with something like that?"

Softly, he said, "It was survival. Just as one needs food, shelter, clothing, water, there is also a need to be wily and endure life. Morgana was especially good at quomodocunquizing."

"I don't—are you making up words now?"

"She was a hustler," he explained. "Once she decided what she wanted, she was very good at talking others into getting it for her."

Olivia looked at her watch and stood. "I am going to turn you."

"Nothing but a piece of meat."

She joked, "I just don't want to overcook you on one side." She untucked the white linens that covered him. "This will be quick. I am a pro at this part."

A slick length of red fabric sewn into a tube shape was pulled from the drawer of the medical table next to his bed. It jingled all of the extra supplies, like syringes, bandages, and kits, as if it were the kitchen junk drawer. She stood over him, pulled his body over to her on his side, dropped the slick fabric flat below his back, and let him down gently. In each step of her process, she would move his arms to a position safely around his torso so as not to get in the way. The smooth fabric allowed her, with little extra effort, to slide his body to a new position on the bed. "When I was little, my mother used to say, 'he who sups with the devil needs a long spoon.'" She took his pillow, fluffed it up, folded it, and returned it to the head of the bed. "Stay away from the devil or you will become like him."

"Morgana wasn't the devil, just devilish. It was a matter of making the best choice at the time," he said.

She moved his body up the bed and lifted his head in a smooth, synchronized movement, resting him gently in a new position.

"You must understand," he added, "one will do nearly anything to live, to stay alive."

With a skill and practice that made it look easy, she lifted the sheet and blanket over him, and they slowly descended as the air escaped beneath, giving the illusion they were floating over him. When they finally landed in a restful state, her quick hands tucked him under the covers to warm him again.

"Viktor, I understand. I have been witness to it. Every day, I see grown men become children at the sight of a needle and fight the urge to move when I am taking blood." She took the red fabric designed to help her turn patients, folded it, and returned it to the drawer. Olivia picked up one of the needles wrapped in its sanitary sealed paper and held it in front of Viktor to see. "Even when it is logical to stay still, not move, and make it hurt less, the needle is no longer a view of health and well-being. The urge to flee, to escape, is huge but shortsighted."

"The power to turn some boys into men and some men into boys," he said.

She set the needle down on top of the table next to his bed and said, "Another quote from your book? Devil or devilish, doing anything to stay alive is an instinct. Having a good life is another thing."

"Yes, yes, shortsighted maybe, but to survive and remain unharmed is at the very core of us."

"Viktor stays with Morgana. He could have run, he could have pushed her overboard and made her swim for it. He had every chance to leave her. Instead, he returned. Was it the gold? The ship? He must have known better."

Viktor thought for a moment and then said, "Men are more romantic than women realize. Women are practical. When a man believes in love, there is no turning back." He watched Olivia move the comfortable chair around his bed to the new side he faced, pick up the book, and continue to read.

∞ 12 ∞

Chapter Nine: Estate

Year 1851
Viktor age 32
Morgana age 29

I T HAD BEEN twelve years since that night in New Orleans. Viktor would still wake hearing the screams of agony and pain from the men of the *Ponthieva* fill his nightmares, the cries in the darkness as the men's bodies contorted and collapsed from the burly, strong sailors to tots no older than a single year, transforming from the flesh wrinkled, sunburned, worn, and traveled to the smooth, soft perfection of infancy. The pain must have been incredible, the fear overpowering.

When nights like this persisted, Morgana would gently stroke his arms, sooth his mind with words, and assure him of the second chance at life they were all given. "It was the best action we could have taken," she would say. "The alternatives were even darker," she would go on to explain.

Still, repetition of this sentiment over the years did not ease his mind. These were good men. These were brave men. They were his friends. What type of man could do something like this to his fellow man? Viktor found this troubled his mind the longer time passed. Even in the days that followed, when he and Morgana traveled the seas with a new crew, seeing the world, seeking adventure, he could never forget. He felt this had hardened him in a way that may be irreversible.

This night, the calming words of Morgana fell flat, so he decided to walk the grounds. She had been a wonderful companion, a good friend, a trusted advisor, and a wonderful lover. She was smart, wily, and, without a moment's doubt, able to jump into any situation and turn it to her favor.

His mind drifted to a time in Marrakesh when she talked her way out of being traded to a sultan. She had once convinced two men at a saloon in San Francisco to fight one another over her to get a head start to their claim. These were years of fun distraction, but none could erase the memories of that night in New Orleans. The two had avoided that haunted city at all costs.

Those years, that night, and the expedition had all paid off in the end. He loved this land he walked. The estate they had purchased was ideal for a man of the sea. It reminded him of growing up in Sweden. The main house sat atop the cliffs overlooking the Atlantic. Acres of tall, sweet-smelling pines surrounded the three-story stone house with a white gravel drive leading from the main road. There were stables for the horses, separate housing for the staff, and a garden where he and Morgana could steal away an afternoon locked hand in hand. From their favorite spot in the garden, they could watch the bay and remember the tales together.

In that bay, anchored just a short distance from the docks, always within sight from that spot, was the *Ponthieva*. This night, he sat in the garden and watched. The white flowers specially picked for the nighttime blossom guided his steps along the path in near luminary brightness. The *Ponthieva* swayed with the waves, bathed in the moon's glow. She needed a new coat of paint after a good scrubbing. She could use a new crew. She needed a new captain, one less sedentary and slow than he. The sleepless nights and years of risks had taken their toll on Viktor.

"Couldn't sleep?" Morgana asked. She joined him as she often did in that spot. "I thought I might find you out here. What is on your mind this night?"

The cool fresh air of the night filled his lungs as he thought of the right words to say. "How much more gold and treasure is enough?"

She laughed. "You once told me you could imagine a lot. Maybe your imagination isn't as grand as you thought."

"We have treasure and then some. How much more do we need? How much more can we carry?"

She sat with him on the bench and took his hand. Gently, she placed it under the cover of her shawl, close against the white nightgown, near to her skin. "Is it the gold that keeps you up? Or the faces of the men who last held it?"

"Both. No matter how many trusted staff we have here, the arms they carry to protect us, I still worry that there will one day be someone faster or stronger to take you away from me."

"Me? You worry about me?"

"You are the only treasure worth protecting; you are my greatest prize."

"I am no man's prize," she whispered. "I may be your wife and lover, but I am no one's to own."

"I cannot imagine losing you," he replied. In a tender tenor, he said, "I can always find more gold, more riches, but not another you."

"That is better." Her hand now combed the hair over his troubled brow. "And what to do with the *Ponthieva*?"

"I do not know. One more adventure? A museum? Sell her to another captain? Those days are best behind me."

"Let us return to bed. Perhaps you can exhaust yourself in my pleasure and find sleep." She stood, his hand in hers, and was drawing him home when he raised the topic proven to spoil her mood.

"Maybe we will be blessed with a child after all this lovemaking."

"Babies." She cringed. "You know I don't want babies. I can't stand the idea of being tied to children. You may make love to me all you want in any way you please, but we are not to have babies."

"You would have a team of caretakers, your choice of nannies, it could be sent away for school, and still you won't have my child."

"I adore you, I love you, and all this is well and good, but I still have to bear the child, carry the child, and be responsible for its life." She stopped before reaching the house to look him in the eyes. "We have talked about this ad nauseam." Her sweetness returned with a smile. "Let us retire to the bedroom without further discussion. We can think of the pleasures of the flesh and not the duties of role and responsibility. Women can do so much more than make babies and bend to man's will. I have a brain as well as breasts."

"Yes, you are correct," Viktor resigned. "I will ravish your body until we are both exhausted, and I will find slumber."

———◦———

It was midday when the two finally woke and were ready for the world. For Viktor, it was the first time he had been able to get a full cycle of deep sleep. For Morgana, it was another night when she slipped between the tingling sensations that touched every bit of her skin and craving for Viktor and the world of dreams, unable to distinguish between the two blurred worlds.

Cleaned and dressed, they were in the middle of a hearty meal when a group of unexpected guests rang at the door. The guests were shown to the visiting parlor by the butler, and the Eriksons were notified.

A group of eight boys dressed in clean but ragged wears sat in the front room, looking at the cups of tea and cookies. They were polite and stood when the Eriksons entered.

"Mr. Erikson, Mrs. Erikson," the leader greeted them.

"Boys," Viktor said. It was a hearty welcome. "What brings you to our home today? Raising money for the church? Selling goods?"

When the door was closed and they were alone, the young man replied, "We are here for the *Ponthieva* and our cut of the gold."

Stunned, Morgana and Viktor looked at one another. It took a moment for the words to sink in. Viktor looked at the eight boys on the verge of manhood. On close inspection, he could see it in the eyes. Gone were the gray hairs, wrinkled lines, and day-old whiskers, but the eyes remained steady, steely, and true. "Captain Durand?"

"Aye," the young captain replied.

"Oh dear Lord," Morgana said. "You're alive. You remember."

"Every detail of every day," Durand snapped.

Viktor looked to the others individually. "Mr. Sinclair?"

"Aye," he replied.

"Mr. Rico?"

"Aye," the young Rico said.

Viktor scanned the faces. He was slow to recognize, in their eyes, that it was the crew that once stood at his side on the *Ponthieva*. "There are only eight of you? Where is Mr. Han? Where is Mr. Turner?" Viktor asked.

"Dead. Both dead. Most of the others too." Durand held tight to a bitter patois in explanation. It was the same hard man trapped in a boy's body. "You left us in an orphanage to fend for ourselves before we could even speak. Han and Turner were taken away the same week. Slaves as best as we could guess. Dead from what we could piece together. Fever caught others. Life happened to the rest."

Viktor fell back into his chair, unable to imagine the years.

"Where's your quick tongue and charming smile now, Mr. Erikson? I can understand the mistakes in the jungle, Han and I drinking the water, but the men? How could you do that to the crew of the *Ponthieva*? They were your brothers."

"How bad was it for you?" Viktor asked.

"Bad is bad any way you cut it," Durand said. "The pain passes, but the memory never fades."

"You remember everything?"

"My life before and this one—every day. I wake up thinking about you, Mr. Erikson, about the deceit you made on my men when this siren called you."

The seven others began to fan out in the room, circling the Eriksons slowly.

"What about your childhood?"

"The survivors stayed tight, looking out for one another when we could, but that first year, learning to talk again, walk again, the mind was there, but the body wouldn't follow. Eventually, we ran that orphanage, worked angles on the streets wherever we could, looking for information, looking for you. We heard about the legends of the *Ponthieva* in Asia, Europe, Africa, and we knew one day, if we waited, we could catch you."

"What is it you want?" Morgana spoke up.

"Just what I said: our cut of the gold and the *Ponthieva*."

"The *Ponthieva* is docked off the shore. Take her . . . she is yours," Morgana stated. "As for the gold, it's gone."

"Gone?!" Durand shouted.

"You are standing in what remains of the spending," she said. "You didn't think all those tales came for free, did you? We spent years going back to find that fountain, to find more gold—never a drop, never an ounce."

"What about Africa?" St. Clair asked.

"The new crew took it all." She looked down in shame. "Took it all and ran. Left us to sail the *Ponthieva* back with only a few we found in port willing to traverse the Atlantic in winter back here, back home."

"Is that right, Mr. Erikson? Money all spent?" Durand asked as he stepped forward.

"You can take what's on the walls, and I have some bank notes in the safe. It's yours considering all the wrong I've done."

"Let's see that safe," Durand said, drawing a pistol from his jacket.

Viktor stood and said, "You won't need that." He turned and walked out of the room, leading the young men. They walked into the library, the one room in the house that was open to all three floors. Each level of books had a ladder leading up to the next level. It was the largest private collection in the Americas and the envy to most who would admire such a thing. Viktor pulled on a velvet rope that rang a bell. He then pulled at the edge of a shelf that turned on a hinge to reveal a hidden safe large enough to walk in. Inside, the wooden shelves of the vault lay empty except for twelve stacks of currency. Individually, he picked up each stack and handed them to St. Clair.

"I am sorry to have done this to you, William," Viktor said, turning to his once closest friend and captain. "I am sorry for what I did to your men."

A look of disgust grew on Durand's face watching this pathetic man hand over the money. With a quick strike, the outpour of rage began. Durand punched Viktor clear across the jaw. He followed with a jab to the nose, causing a loud crack as it broke and a spray of blood to fly. The brown droplets hit the Georgian rug before Viktor joined them, lying face up.

"Where is the water?" Durand said, slowly pressing the toe of his boot into Viktor's cheek. "I know you kept a flask."

"Stop it!" Morgana cried. "Stop it! You're going to kill him."

"Killing's too good for this one," Durand said.

Unsteadily, Viktor's hand moved from his side and pointed above the fireplace.

Durand's eyes found it in an instant. The polished silver flask nearly glowed with a vibrant life of its own in the case on the mantel. He felt a fool for not having seen it before, hiding it in plain sight. With a point and a nod of the captain's head, Rico followed the unspoken instructions from the captain to retrieve it.

In hand, Durand turned the cap, feeling the grit of metal on metal as it twisted. "You wanted to know what it was like? I'll let you know exactly what it felt like." Durand grabbed at Viktor's throat, forcing his mouth open, and turned the flask, pouring the water over him and washing away the blood. What landed in his mouth was enough. The involuntary contortions began, and Viktor started to scream in agony. Durand stood over his body to watch and take pleasure in the proceedings he once suffered, deciding this was full payment in return of what he had done.

Bursting through the doors were fifteen men with arms drawn, each with beaded aim at the heads of the remaining crew of the *Ponthieva*.

"My personal guards," Morgana said.

"The bell," Durand replied. The look on his face showed an appreciation for the subtle deception.

"They have what they've come for. Take them to the *Ponthieva*," Morgana instructed.

The head guard raised his pistol to Durand's head and said, "Sir."

Durand, followed by the others, proceeded out the doors. Above the cries of pain from Viktor writhing on the floor, she could hear the exterior doors open and the men march away. The cries of pain transformed into the cries of a baby. She picked up her baby Viktor and swaddled him the shirt now too large. His cries began to subside in her arms. His breathing steadied.

"I guess there is no getting away from raising babies," she said. Stepping into the empty vault, she pressed a hidden latch on the shelf. With a click, the shelf moved away from the wall to reveal an immense windowless brick room. It too included shelves for money, and these were stacked high with currency. Bars of gold lined the walls in neat piles. The floor was solid and sure with stone to support all the weight. Unique items lay open in the vault, like rare statues and a line of rare paintings. Jewels filled vases or were set in jewelry. The entire room seemed vibrant with the little light that entered from the open secret door.

With her free hand, Morgana removed a few bundles of wrapped bank notes and closed the door. She placed these down where the twelve stacks of bait previously sat. She said to her baby Viktor, "At least you will have the best care and nannies."

In the distance, she could hear the bells of the *Ponthieva* ringing out in preparation for departure.

❧ 13 ❧

Chapter Ten: Testing the Water

Year 1852
Viktor age 14 months
Morgana age 29

BABY VIKTOR GAVE Morgana goosebumps. It was an ill chill that started at the base of her neck and worked its way through the rest of her body slowly. He would sit silently, watching her. Morgana knew from what Durand explained that he understood, or at least she believed he did. At first, the baby Viktor would struggle to speak, she could see attempts to form words, but the motor skills of an infant could not keep pace with his adult mind. Knowing him, knowing how he thought, she could tell he was planning and plotting behind those adorable eyes and rosy cheeks.

He looked more Nordic as a child than his adult self, with a long torso and strawberry-blond hair. She knew in time he would eventually change to a dark blond, muscular piece of man who could satisfy her every desire. That longing burned in her. It filled her dreams. She wanted so much to have Viktor back—with her, inside her—that at times it would bring her to tears.

It was this alteration between the eerie moments she caught his gaze and the lonely times she couldn't bear to be near him that she began to take precautions.

First, she took the flask that was emptied onto Viktor and parts from the other full flask of the water of life collected until the two were of equal measure. She wanted to know more about the effects of this water. What were the properties that made it so unique? How much would it take to duplicate the outcome? Were the results consistent? Or could they be altered in some way? With all of these questions and no one to talk to, she realized she was her father's daughter.

Under the guidance of a pharmacist she had met at a social gathering in Manhattan and the guise of a fussy baby needing to be fed additional liquids for hydration, she purchased a device called a pipette. To her surprise, the expensive item turned out to be a long glass tube that she could place into a liquid, apply her finger to the top end, and allow for drops of that liquid to fall under reasonable control. In her hands, she recalled it was something her father would use when he worked at the university. With care, she was able to take this long glass tube and cut it into a more manageable length, one that could fit into her purse or coat pocket.

Hares and rabbits caught on the estate would squeal for a few moments before transforming back to leverets and kits. Larger mammals reacted similarly, a horse retuning to a colt, a ram to a cosset. No matter the size or weight, a single drop into a liquid consumed would change that mammal back to its infant version.

The water they'd found was powerful: the results were consistent, and the outcomes were predictable.

Morgana's summer of testing came to a close when she decided to take a trip back to the city. Viktor was in good care with the nanny. The estate was in the hands of trusted staff. She left in her carriage with three private guards, not disclosing her true plans to Viktor.

She was no stranger to the danger of a shipping yard. Few men could actually put fear in her heart after the tyrants she had met. The docks and the roughness about them were a place she felt familiar and comfortable. Calls and advances from sailors were a reminder that she was a desirable woman after having spent months alone, longing for her Viktor.

Some were smelly, fresh from the seas. Others were unshaven and covered in fleas. There was one man who was perfect, drunk in an ally, propped up on something unseen, but swayed like the heavy seas in a galley. She approached him demurely, tickling his delight, and then flicked her finger. He tipped his hat and said, "Good night." Before she reached her third step, a cry called out. Clutching his head, he gurgled, "Help."

No aid was given. She was testing the water. Morgana was exploring as a scientist's daughter.

After two weeks in Manhattan, Morgana returned to her Viktor, satisfied. She had left behind her a trail of growing headlines about abductions. Men of power, means, and the working class had all been reported missing in a short period of time, no trace of struggle or bodies recovered. Just vanished from the face of the earth.

In an unrelated article, the *Brooklyn Daily Eagle* reported that a surprising number of abandoned children had been discovered in recent weeks. The article went on to support the workhouse systems of Europe to discourage those too lazy to support a family or follow through on the commitments of poor decisions.

Morgana laughed when reading this aloud to Viktor. "They could not have gotten it more wrong."

Viktor was only able to look at her with that chilling stare. It seemed judgmental in the moment.

"I am only doing this for you, for us," she said. "I need to understand the impact this has. I need to know how it works."

Baby Viktor looked at her. His weak muscles had become strong enough in her absence to hold himself up and provide partial mobility. Much of his effort turned him in circles on the floor, but it was progress.

"Viktor, I miss you. I miss your hands on me."

Morgana's second concern after the water was about continuity. All the things they had fought for, collected, and won could all be taken away. She needed to be certain that the treasures would never be transferred out of her ownership or lost. So, she consulted the best legal minds in Manhattan and Boston to help her draft an incorruptible document that would follow her wishes faithfully. She needed something that would keep all the possessions, property, and belongings under her control and ownership until Viktor was a man again. Or if the unthinkable were to happen to Viktor, she needed to ensure she would not need to fend for herself in the world.

Morgana began to spend large amounts of time away from Viktor following these interests. With no real means to communicate complex ideas, a fear of infidelity began to grow in his mind.

When she returned to tell him about the advice and documents being created by some of the leading minds to keep them both safe from scoundrels, his mind would always question the other things those men might be giving her. And when she went on about the rallies and support for Susan B. Anthony and Elizabeth Stanton, he thought something more nefarious might be afoot. As Morgana explained the formal trust she had built to anonymously support the ideas and concerns of women, baby Viktor became disheartened by the suspensions that had been brewing inside him which she continued to feed, so he crawled away to his room, frustrated by the limitations of his new life.

That first year was the most difficult period for Viktor and Morgana.

∞ 14 ∞

Prescribed

Year 2053
Olivia age 25

"I CAN'T REMEMBER THE *Ponthieva*," Viktor said.

She noticed this as a pattern. He tended to say this when the pain medication's time release was activated. Her role as that beacon through the fog of drugs faded between those times he was lucid and conversational and those moments his mind was adrift in a sea of the unconscious.

Olivia did not know what to make of this statement he repeated. The man in the bed she called Viktor was certainly a pleasant and charming man to speak with. He could remember the details of the fiction she was reading him with considerable insight, and it was clear he knew the tale. His inability to separate this fiction from what might be his real life pointed her to the conclusion that his brain injury must be more severe than she knew. St. John's was an ideal location for an injury like this one, yet the doctor said there was little they could do. Under that bandage could be something foul she did not want to see. In her studies, she recalled a time when surgeons would make one small cut that severed the lobes, lobotomizing the patient and providing radical changes to personality. This might be part of that deeper unseen injury. He might only recall the book. He might believe that he is Viktor and has lost his true identity. Her role, her priority, was to make certain he was comfortable and was not alone.

"Are you Viktor? Viktor Erikson?" Olivia asked.

"Yes, Viktor," he mumbled.

"Is Morgana your wife?"

"Morgana, wife, daughter, lover, the water." His eye floated in his socket to find her. "Is she here? Morgana?"

"No. I am Olivia. You are at St. John's hospital. Do you remember?"

"St. John's, yes."

"I think the automated drip on your pain medication kicked in again. You are going to be a little fuzzy, but you'll feel no pain."

"Call her. Morgana Erikson. Bring water."

It seemed difficult to believe that the story she had been reading to him was somehow true or partially true. It seemed too amazing to be real.

Olivia turned when she heard the knock at the door.

"Pardon me, are you Olivia?" a man asked from the doorway.

"I am."

"I'm Detective Jimmy Panadero," he explained. "I've been assigned to this case. You said this man is Viktor Erikson?"

"I believe so."

"He came in as a John Doe from the car accident earlier, right?"

"That is correct."

"What made you think that this is Viktor Erikson?"

"Well, his name was inscribed in this book he brought in, and there have been moments when he has talked and said his name was Viktor," she said.

The detective stepped over to Olivia. He smelled like coffee and that glow of body odor one gets from sitting in a car too long. "Sir," Jimmy started, "can you tell me your name?"

"Viktor Erikson," he whispered.

"Do you know where you are?"

"St. John's."

"Do you know what year it is?"

"1852," Viktor said.

Jimmy looked to Olivia for an answer.

"The medication just kicked in. But that's the year in the chapter of the book I am reading to him—1852."

Jimmy sighed. "Well, two out of three is pretty close for a guy in his state. What do you think?"

Olivia shrugged her shoulders. "I'm not sure what to think. He is an older man who was hit by a truck. I may not have gotten my name or location right if I were in his condition."

Jimmy stood and walked to the door. With a tilt of his head, he indicated that Olivia should follow to have a more private conversation. Just outside the door, Jimmy leaned in close and said, "There is the Viktor Erikson on the board of directors, and that Viktor is an old guy. Could be him. His daughter, Morgana Erikson, is also on the board."

"Daughter?" she asked.

"Yeah, says here, daughter, late twenties, part of that Manhattan scene, I guess."

"Oh."

"Well, I've reached out to her—left a message—and to some of the other board members to see if they know how to contact her or to come down to help verify that this is the same Viktor Erikson. How much longer will he hold out?"

"I have no idea. He seems to listen to me read but fades out from time to time when I stop."

"Well, keep reading to him, keep his mind active. We might be able to get someone here before, well, you know."

"Yeah, I know."

"Okay, well, here's my card. Phone is there at the bottom."

"Thank you."

"You, ah, can call that number any time, day or night, whatever you need," Jimmy added.

"Thank you." She could tell he had stopped thinking about the case as he looked at her in that way men were obvious about. She didn't mind. She was looking rather rough tonight.

"Are you new here? I don't think I've seen you here before."

"New to the area, yes."

"Well, if you need a friend, want a cup of coffee—my number, bottom of card."

"Thank you, Detective," she said.

"Call me," Jimmy said before walking down the hallway to the elevator.

Olivia returned to Viktor's side, dropping the business card into her purse for later if needed. "Where were we, Viktor? Were you fighting the leviathan?"

"No, that comes later." He shared a drug-induced smile.

"Really?"

"You will have to keep reading to find out."

"Okay, funny man, I am starting to see your humor here. That's a good thing. You may be getting your strength back. Do you feel hungry?"

"Just thirsty."

She looked at him with curiosity and gave him a sip from the straw. Water was starting to mean something entirely different the more she continued to read through the book. "Viktor, who is Autor Widmor?"

"A Polish author."

"And he wrote this book?"

"I don't remember him, but Morgana told me about him."

"Morgana told you about Autor Widmor?"

"She told me we met him when we visited Warsaw during a summer in Europe. We would spend nearly every night at a pub, drinking and telling stories. He was always taking notes, asking questions, and writing. He sent us each a copy of his book. At the front, you can see his signature has faded."

She paged to the front of the book, and in small writing, on the third page, were the following words:

"Sometimes eraser marks on a page mean more than what's written." —Autor Widmor

"He said it was on a small press. I think they called it a vanity press in those days."

"Do you remember what he looked like?"

"Not really. When I close my eyes, I see tall, lean man with a big curled mustache," he described. "But my memory is not very good."

"So you have said."

"Please read. Please continue," he urged.

"Sure." She explained, "When we last left Viktor, the babies he abandoned in New Orleans had grown to be men and were taking revenge for the pain, stealing the gold, and abandoning them."

"That isn't where we left off, and that isn't what happened," he said.

"You were paying attention. How would you explain what happened?"

Slowly, in his tiny voice, Viktor explained, "They were taken to a place where they could be cared for, not abandoned."

"Yes, but they didn't have a choice in the matter."

"We rarely get to choose our path, Olivia. Most of our lives are reactions to others or events. Those men were given a chance at another life while keeping the lessons from the last. You care for people every day, my dear. Do they all get the best care? Do they have a choice in what happens to them?"

"Not all, no. We make the best choices to prescribe care."

"Prescribe care. If a child is in a bad home, we move them to a better one. Some doctors prescribe medication and others physical therapy for similar ailments."

"Well, yes, I suppose."

"Those men were given the chance to live longer, yet they blamed the same man who gave them that gift for a poor second life, but it was their life to live, not his. Not all evil is madness."

"I think these men were mad about the gold."

"These particular men loved gold. Do you always get a thing because you love it more? Feel you deserve it more?"

"I guess not."

"They took their revenge, they took the *Ponthieva*, and in exchange, they left me with a second chance to live life. It was up to me to live it."

❧ 15 ❧

Chapter Eleven: Drafted Plans

Year 1852
Viktor age 16 months
Morgana age 30

I T HAD COME to no surprise of anyone on the estate that the first word from the baby's mouth was "no." Viktor had been brooding away for months on his own, trying to force the muscles of his little body to comply with his will. In the prior three months, he had also been forcing himself to walk by holding on to the items in a room. Just when he thought he had conquered the ability of balance, his body would grow more and he would have to learn the nuances of each step again. It was a constant struggle that had, on more than one occasion, brought him to tears. The staff just thought it was normal of the baby to finally cry this way; it scared Morgana to see him like this.

With the first few words of "no" and "yes," the two could finally start to communicate again. Their long-term plans and well-being were the first topics she wanted to discuss.

"The lawyers," she explained in privacy, "have drafted this document that passes all control to the other in cases of a chance occurrence or unavoidable accident. It is the best way they could describe what has happened. You see, turning into a child isn't the same as dying. You are still here, you are still you, but there are still decisions that need to be made."

"You tell?" he asked.

"I did. They didn't believe me. They thought I was a loon. In fact, both said that my mental state would negate such a document, if challenged, just by requesting such a document. But the money I was willing to pay for them to write it compelled them."

"Yes," Viktor said.

"In talking with each of them at length, it gave me an idea. An idea I am not sure you will like or understand, but it is good if you will listen."

"Yes."

"You know I am not one who is interested in babies, having or raising them. Still, this situation we are in where we have the best care and nannies available certainly helps." She took a moment to gather her thoughts. The way she explained it in her mind seemed so eloquent and persuasive. "I think that you and I should take turns drinking this water."

A puzzled look came across Viktor's face that she couldn't help but find adorable.

She went on. "Consider this: I am raising you as my child by view of the outside world. We are both getting older at the same rate. There will be this period of time when you are a child and I am an adult. When you are a young man, there will be a point when I start to get old and unattractive to you."

"No," Viktor said sweetly.

"It's true. You may love me, but I will get old and wrinkled and you will be young again, seeking adventure like when we met." She lifted him and set him in her lap. "When I get too old, I will drink the water and become a child and you can raise me. Our love could last as long as we have the water, taking turns, and there would be decades when we could be lovers together. Just think of it."

She could see by his expression he was giving it careful consideration. "More," he said.

She smiled and added details. "In all of my experiments—"

"Bad," he interrupted.

"Necessary," she said.

"Bad."

"I will not argue the past with you. It happened. In all of my experiments, they all reverted to roughly that age under one, yet never too young. No matter the dose, the potency was the same." She reached over to the table to retrieve a document. It contained a table with ages. "Look here, I did some calculations to our ages. This column is your age, this column mine. We could take turns raising one another. There would be periods of time the two of us would look like parent and child and other periods we could publically be a couple."

"Yes," Viktor said.

She pointed to the table. "When you turn this age, I will drink the water and you will raise me." Looking to him again, she said, "You must understand, I love you, Viktor, and I am trusting you with my life, to raise me, to care for me, to spend eternity with you. I need you to feel the same in order for this to work between us."

His little hand took hers. He pulled her close and kissed her. "Yes."

Understanding

Year 2053
Olivia age 25

"Ew," SHE SAID finishing the last line.

"What is it?"

"That is so creepy. The little . . . and she is—ew."

"You find it *awkward* when babies kiss their mothers," he said.

"No, that is totally different. She is not his mother, and he is not her child."

"And while his body is that of an infant, his mind is that of a man. She sees him as that man."

"Ew, no. It's still creepy."

He turned his head in indifference to her opinion.

She could see that her reaction had hurt his feelings or been taken poorly, so she said, "I find it awkward that there are some actions you can make as a child that are totally unacceptable as an adult, like dressing up as a ballerina or a pretty princess in public."

He turned his head to face her direction. The smile on his face was large. "Sitting on someone's lap."

She returned the smile, seeing that he had caught on. "Running through the front yard sprinkler naked."

"Climbing into bed with your parents and calling them 'mommy' and 'daddy.'"

"Having a crush on a ten-year-old," she said.

"Shitting your pants."

She laughed. "Oh, that is very common in my line of work, no matter the age."

"I suppose there are many social norms acceptable in the right light," he said.

"I guess so."

"For these two, behind closed doors, they were still the strapping sailor and the beautiful Southern belle. No matter what others saw, said, or thought."

"Maybe that is part of owning such a large estate and having a staff— you can do anything you like."

"Nearly."

"Should I keep reading?"

"Only if you want to know the ending."

"I do," she said and then opened the book to where they left off.

Chapter Twelve: The Manor

Year 1863
Viktor age 13
Morgana age 41

D URING THOSE ELEVEN years, Morgana proved to have a keen mind for investments. She continued the financial support of the efforts to empower women from the safety of anonymity, and when Viktor asked her to put money into the areas of steel and manufacturing, she found the right people.

Since taking the water, Viktor no longer had nightmares. He no longer felt the guilt of having forced others to transform. It was a pain that he could forget and believed that the living crew of the *Ponthieva* would too. It was the bitterness of that first year that lingered. He imagined Rico, St. Clair, Durand, and the others having no ability to say anything that first year and, instead, savoring the ideas of revenge in silence, waiting for the right moment to strike. He considered the matter resolved. He had Morgana. He had the real treasure.

Desire appeared to Viktor in a dream. It woke him immediately. He sprang from his bed, washed, and then found himself drawn down the hallway to Morgana's room. Silently, he joined her in bed, providing small kisses along her neck to her lips, and began to stroke all the places she liked best.

She stirred from slumber. "Is this a dream?"

"No, this is real, my love," he replied.

Her moans of pleasure followed. The two were ideally matched to enjoy the experience. He had the endurance and strength of a young man with the skill and patience of his true age. She had an uncontrollable urge to grab and draw him near. It felt as if something had been missing from her all these years. Compelled to fill the void inside her, she knew his penetration was the only thing in the world that could make her feel whole. When they finished, she felt empty, as if withdrawing took away that unifying force that kept them in orbit of one another. Lying in his arms, watching his chest rise and fall, her only desire was to start once more and feel whole with him again.

Days of passion turned into weeks until the two were exhausted and devoid of new ideas in June of 1863.

"The fools!" Viktor yelled.

"What? What is it?" she asked.

Breakfast spilled across the table in his rage and the newspaper in hand crumpled. "Napoléon III sent troops to Mexico. They are in Veracruz."

"I don't understand. Why are you so angry?"

"They are a week's ride from the fountain. They are so close. First it was the Spanish and now Napoléon III. They must know it's there. The power-hungry fool." He fell back into his chair.

She took the paper from his hand gingerly. He had been quick to emotion the last few days. She suspected it was what most men had gone through at this age. She did not suspect it to be so intense outside the bedroom. "Look here, it says that they are opening trade with Mexico," she explained.

"Silver, he is after the silver mines. When they turn south, they will find the pyramids, more than we had time for, more gold, the fountain."

"There was no more gold. The map—"

"The map? The drawing you and your father made? That sketch couldn't have been very accurate. We were rushed! There was no time to get it all. It was dark—we may have missed something on that wall."

"I don't like you like this. Your mood is too sour for me. What is your trouble? Why are you behaving this way?"

"I do not know," he said with a huff. "I do not know. I need . . ."

"You need what?"

"I need to leave this house. I feel confined."

"You feel confined on this estate? Ride a horse. Sail your boat. Chop down a tree. There is nothing here to confine you outside of the eighteen rooms."

"It is not enough."

"It is not enough? What more could you need or want? Do you want adventure? Find a cause; there must be hundreds. If you can't find one, join the army. There is a terrible war of aggression being waged on the South. Do you want to go west? To Europe? What do you want, my love? It is yours."

"I do not know. I just know this is not enough."

She felt hurt by his words and tried not to show it. "We have enough water to last us both several lifetimes. We need to trust one another. We need to be true."

The heat of his emotions passed just as quickly as it came. He knew he had said too much already. "Oh, my love, it is enough. You are more than enough for me. You are my sun, my moon, and my stars." He took her hand and kissed her cheek. "I do feel confined. I need to do something, travel, and see new places."

"I would like nothing more. Should I pack for Mexico?"

"I was thinking I might go on my own."

Her face seemed to melt at the suggestion, taut and happy at the idea of travel, sagging and weary at the idea of being alone.

"Just for a while," he said in reply to her expression. "I have no friends, no one to talk to outside of you. I could use some perspective, a change, something different."

"Am I that old to you? That grotesque?"

"That is not it at all, and you know it. I will take you right now to prove it," he said, and she wished he would. Instead, he continued, "I am looking for someone to . . . I don't know how to put it."

"You are looking for Captain Durand."

"Yes, not him, but someone like him."

"You need someone who will fight and not seduce an opponent. You want a person good with a gun and quick with a blade who has your back."

"Yes, yes, that's right."

"I understand."

"Don't be so dour, Morgana. You traveled without me, and I didn't say a thing."

"You *couldn't* say a thing."

"Aside from that, you were in New York doing your experiment, attending parties, or in Boston doing business and meeting new people. I have been here for more than a decade."

"Go, go, pack your things, go. Find yourself a bold new venture and meet your new William Durand while I wait here for pirates to raid our house, longing for your return."

"Why are you being dramatic? There are a slew of men outside these doors with guns and more at the edges of the land on watch. You are as safe here as anywhere."

She turned away from him to look out the window and hide the pain she felt. "What will you do? Where will you go?"

"If I had a ship, I could be a privateer to run goods into Savannah."

"You would be shot, if caught."

"I could be a railway man."

"You seem to be forgetting something, my dear."

"What?"

"You look like a teenage boy. Unsupervised and with documents that show you should be an old man, you would be grabbed on the streets and taken to march with the Union."

"I want no part in war," he said. "I want to feel alive, and war is certain death."

The two were at an impasse. She could not always keep him safe. He could not always be free. It reminded him of the hold she had on him, first noticed in Philadelphia when he wanted to confide in Professor Leidy. How that hold had tightened over the years.

"I am going to go riding," he said.

Chapter Thirteen: The Azores Islands

Year 1872
Viktor age 22
Morgana age 50

IN 1872, THE two made love one last time before it was Morgana's turn to drink the water. He was twenty-two, she fifty. The week before had been filled with arrangements. Morgana hired caregivers and nannies to care for a baby girl she described as her cousin whose parents had been tragically lost. The guards were provided a generous severance with no hard feelings on departure and former Pinkertons hired to run the new guards of the estate.

After that final night of passion, Morgana took the glass rod and placed the single droplet of water on her tongue to transform.

Something inside of Morgana always felt the need to care for Viktor as a baby. She had a desire to check in on his state often. These were natural feelings of taking care for baby Viktor even though he was not her child.

Viktor, however, did not share this desire. While Morgana was a beautiful baby, she did not need attention or entertainment. She found ways of her own to occupy her mind. A staff of nannies was quick to intercede and maintain her daily needs around the clock in different shifts so no one person became overwhelmed.

Viktor found himself on extended holidays in the city that summer, knowing she was in the best care. He joined the Union Club, where he thought men of like minds might socialize. Many of the members treated him poorly, thinking him too young, and the stories of the older members seemed too embellished for his liking.

After returning to the estate to check on Morgana, he explained that he had decided to take on with a ship out of New York to feed this desire he had long felt.

A year later, Viktor returned, and Morgana watched him drink with abandon. There was hardly a morning when she didn't see him without a glass in hand. By day's end, the whole bottle would spill in his stupor. Eventually, the few hours when he could stand were unpleasant-smelling rants of sadness and misery. It was as if the staff were caring for two children.

Talking came easier for Morgana. It started at an earlier age and didn't stop.

Viktor woke one morning with baby Morgana sitting on top of him and talking away, fueling the pains of a hangover that had been building for months. "Get off me," he said.

"No," she insisted.

"What is it you want? Leave me alone," he insisted.

"Why?"

"You wouldn't understand," he said to the stern face of the child. From her stubborn expression, he knew he could not convince her otherwise. In this state of mind, he was too weak with the effects drunkenness to resist. "I don't know how you live with yourself after the cruelty you inflicted on Manhattan while 'testing' your theory of the water."

"What happened?"

"I used the water on a whole crew of men and killed them all." The grief gurgled in the back of his throat as if he were going to be sick admitting it.

"So long ago," she said.

"No, no, this isn't the *Ponthieva*. It happened again . . . on the *Mary Celeste*," he explained.

"You were on the *Mary Celeste*?"

"Yes," he sobbed. "I was trapped, caught by my past—St. Clair and Rico were on the ship too. I put the water from the fountain in the fresh water supply and found the ship nearly empty in a storm. Then, the last of the crew slipped into the sea, unable to fend for themselves."

She watched his outpouring of emotions over the matter and began to understand the deep sorrow he must have felt. It explained why he had taken up drinking.

"I don't understand how you can live with the actions you have taken with so few repercussions while I am constantly making these mistakes that bring death and despair. Men seek me out for revenge. I am a bad man who does bad things!" he proclaimed.

Crawling off him to lie by his side, Morgana stroked his hair with her hand as she had in the past to ease his mind late at night. "You are not bad," she said. "You did what was needed. I will do what I must to survive."

Soothed by the calming words and feeling safe and slightly sober in the bed they shared, he explained what had transpired during their time apart.

In the fall of 1872, Viktor had joined the crew of the *Mary Celeste*, a merchant brigantine that had sailed under an American flag and the command of Captain Benjamin Briggs, who was known for being very cautious in the selection of men to join his crew. All were seasoned professionals, trusted and sure. Viktor, while looking young, had impressed the captain with his skills and knowledge.

After leaving from Pier 50 with a haul full of denatured alcohol, the weather for the voyage had become a concern, so they'd anchored off Staten Island. It was during this final stop before departure that a small craft with two last-minute additions had boarded the *Mary Celeste*. In an instant, he had recognized one man as St. Clair a aaand the other as Rico. They had not seen Viktor when boarding, but the vessel was not one large enough to stay hidden the entire voyage.

In the moment, Viktor had considered two options. First, he could have jumped ship. He would have needed to do this immediately without thinking about the consequences. Looking over the railing as the ship started to draw anchor and move out with the tide, he had known the water would be too strong and cold for the swim; he would have surely drowned or frozen.

His second option had been to hide, taking assignments in the lower decks or in the sails where the two were not likely see him. This plan had worked well during the early days of the passage. It had allowed him time to grow a beard and alter his appearance as much as possible. St. Clair had even passed by him once in such a hurry that they bumped arms without noticing who he was.

It had been a clear day on deck when Rico had spotted him from a distance. Rico had glowered at Viktor for a good while without action, unchanged, attempting to figure out where he knew that frame and familiar face. Viktor had focused on the task at hand, looking up to see Rico engage St. Clair in conversation while keeping a careful eye.

The risks had been too high, the danger too great, so Viktor had done what he believed he needed to do in order to survive. Artfully, Viktor had made his way to the fresh water reserves and emptied the small vial he carried for emergencies.

He had felt the heavy hand on his shoulder just hours later. "Didn't think I would see you again, Mr. Erikson," St. Clair had said.

Rico had been quick with the stick as Viktor's world had gone black. He'd awoken in the brig. Iron and wood on three sides with the hull on a fourth, it had made for a tight prison cell.

He had been alone for a day when the drive of hunger and thirst had pushed him to attempt an escape. For hours, he had worked uninterrupted on the wooden door to force it open. With no response at the loud noises of his work, he had put all he had into the effort until it finally moved. There had been a crack of wood when he'd realized the tossing of the seas.

Thunder in the distance had sounded with a rush of wind. He had continued to work at the door until the hole he'd created was large enough for him to squeeze through.

The *Mary Celeste* had started to list as if no one were at her command. Violently, she had landed back the other direction into a wave. Each step had been an effort down the corridor and up the steps to the main deck.

On deck, he had looked starboard and he seen three naked infants slip overboard into the darkness of the stormy seas. The sins he had committed were unimaginable in that moment. The entire crew had drunk from the fresh water reserves before rushing to the deck to face the tempest, not knowing when they might be able to touch another drop.

Reports of finding the derelict ship adrift off the Azores Islands had made their way around the world before Viktor had been able to book passage and return home to Morgana. Details of the discovery were accurate as to where and how he had left her: sails partially up, well provisioned, wheel lashed, and the lifeboat missing as Viktor had rowed ashore on his own. Questions about the crew and what had happened grew. Some had said it was a sea spout, giant squid, or seismic anomaly that took her men. Others had blamed the owners in a deception or foul play for insurance.

One thing Viktor knew over his lifetimes was that the sea has no end to its mysteries or tales. None would suspect that he had heedlessly killed each man by turning them into defenseless infants before a deadly storm.

❧ 19 ❧

Questions

Year 2053
Olivia age 25

OLIVIA PICKED UP her phone and started to search for the *Mary Celeste* while the medications kicked in for Viktor again. History hadn't been one of her best subjects in school. Her strategy had been to memorize what was needed for tests and class discussion, never really learning about things of the past.

Her device explained that the *Mary Celeste* was a ghost ship discovered in the Atlantic missing all her crew, with no signs of life or struggle. The mystery of what happened had been highly publicized and controversial in its day. It was one of the great unsolved mysteries of the sea.

This only verified to Olivia that Autor Widmor had been careful to include historical events in his writing. If this were Viktor, the Viktor in the book, the man would have to be over an unachievable age of two hundred years. This book she was reading was some strange combination historical fiction with a touch of biography someone who could live for generations might keep. This tale of Viktor and Morgana showed that the experience of keeping such a tale would be helpful if one were injured or lost without the help of the other.

Olivia started to ask her device more questions about historical markers in the book. If parts of were true, couldn't more of this be true? Could someone have found the answer to immortality and kept it a secret for generations? She needed to talk to someone other than Viktor, someone who would not think her crazy to pose these types of questions and was smart enough to think through these concepts. Who was the biggest geek she knew?

She stepped into the bathroom and said into her phone, "Call David Little." In seconds, David's face appeared on the screen.

"Hey, Olivia! How are things?"

"Good, thanks. I need your opinion on something as a pharmacist."

"All right. Where are you? I haven't seen you around in weeks."

"I had to change hospitals."

"What?"

"Yeah, long story. I had to change things up after some personal things happened," she said.

"Sorry to hear that. I always enjoyed having lunch in the cafeteria with you."

"Yeah, we should do that again soon."

"What's on your mind that you needed chemistry help?"

"Has anyone ever discovered the ability to stop or reverse ageing?"

"What? Like the fountain of youth?" he asked.

Her voice waned with doubt. "Something like that, but it doesn't have to be that."

"Well, the fountain of youth is a myth," he said, as if it were obvious to anyone. "It's only a tourist attraction in Florida. That whole Ponce de León thing is fundamentally off the mark of reality. It's really only popularized in North America."

"Really?"

"Yeah, I don't know that the guy ever found anything. But if you are asking about chemical discoveries to live longer, appear younger, there has been a lot of money going into that research for years. Hell, our average lifespan as humans is way longer than it has ever been, even twenty or fifty years ago."

"Healthier living, better medicine, antibiotics—I get that. Any one thing that helps with that?"

"Not that I know of. Lots of little things combined, but no one thing."

"Hmmm," she said.

David filled the silence. "You know, in my mind, if there were a fountain of youth, it's less likely that it would be a chemical thing."

"What do you think it would be?"

"It would have to be an anomaly in space and time. It would be a hot spot, like under the earth's crust. There are these thin parts in the earth's crust that make hot spots on the surface. Yellowstone Park is on top of one. Over centuries, the crust moves, the hot spot stays in place, and a series of these thermals pop up. The Hawaiian Islands are like that: a series of volcanic islands made from this hot spot rolling over the planet's surface for centuries."

"And the fountain of youth would be like that how?"

"The anomaly in space and time—you wade in it, and it makes you younger or keeps you young. Time won't change there because of it."

"Would you be able to take it with you?" Olivia asked.

"I don't know. It's just a theory. I guess so. The atoms and particles in that time and space would somehow be impacted by this anomaly, and you could carry that with you, consume it. Sure, why not? I may be thinking of an episode of *Star Trek*, but if you're talking about the fountain of youth, why not talk about *Star Trek*?"

"Interesting idea. Thanks for your time, David."

"Could you imagine the vanity?"

"How do you mean?"

"If you were eternally young, the 'God Complex' you would have? If you think that doctors are vain, imagine someone who lives forever or just several lifetimes. They would start to toy with people like they were playthings, interfere with lives just for the fun of it."

"I never gave it much thought."

"I sure wouldn't want to meet anyone with that ability," he said. "I would be taken advantage of pretty easily. I am a sucker for those kinds of things—guess I am a romantic. You?"

"A romantic? I don't know, David. Thank you very much for your help."

"No problem, any time. Call me later. We can catch up, do lunch."

"Sounds good," she said. The phone disconnected, and David's face disappeared.

Viktor called out as best as he could, "Is David your boyfriend?"

"No, no, he is just someone I used to know," she said, returning to his side.

"I see," Viktor said. "I find it awkward when people don't come out and ask the question they want to ask for fear of hurting someone's feelings."

Her chuckle was one of uncertainty. "Are we still playing that game?"

"If you like."

"Viktor, what does the title of this book mean? *The Ethics of Immortality*?"

With his good eye closed, he continued, "I am not sure if old Autor was being crafty or trying to jab at me." His head turned on the pillow to get a better view of her with his now opened eye. "If your friend David were able to make a potion that kept people alive longer, would he give it to everyone? Or would he keep it for the ones he loved? Share it with the few that he could put up with for all those extra years?"

"I don't know."

"I don't know either, but I suspect that having this power might go to one's head. It might not be a gift to the world. Immortality has nothing to do with the quality of life, just the longevity of it. What good is it if your body operates forever but you are in a coma?"

"Not very good," Olivia agreed.

"A long life for everyone means fewer generations that follow or suffering from overpopulation. I suppose if your life is miserable with overpopulation, suicides would happen more and you would need to allow for euthanasia."

"I guess I never thought of that."

"There is a reason humans don't live long: we are selfish and greedy. A long life would be best for those few we love and want to see every day, not the assholes we can't stand."

"Ugh, there are a few people I would not want to see every day forever."

"Olivia, as I grow older, the more reflection I have spent on those I have spent my life with, questioning the things done and who I was with when doing them. With time, reflection, and experience, I wonder if what I did was right, but I did my best at the moment. I thought I was doing the right thing at the time."

Olivia sat for a moment, considering his words, picked up the book, and began to read where she left off.

❧ 20 ❧

Chapter Fourteen: The Owl Night Club

Year 1885
Viktor age 35
Morgana age 14

IT WAS TOO difficult to stay with Morgana on the estate. She looked fourteen and he thirty-five. Their professional staff remained loyal, such as her primary nurse, Elsie Smith, and his main assistant, Alaric Bichel, but others could easily describe the family they cared for as being eccentric. The way the child treated Viktor was, at best, awkward if they were not related and bordered on criminal if they were. The eccentric nature of families with this type of money was not original to the Eriksons. This speculation could have easily been covered up with a simple lie from Morgana or Viktor, yet they remained silent on the matter.

Word of the wonders from the West had made their way back east. After seeing Buffalo Bill's Wild West show, Morgana became enchanted with the romance of the West. It was full of adventure and opportunity, something they both desired. So, in the winter of 1885, they decided to commission a private railway car to travel west. It was a project the two could work on together. Ideas would blossom from discussions and dreams. Nearly every day, they would visit the car as it was being built. Craftsmen would alter items on the spot, add amenities, or test the concepts brought to them earlier.

By the spring, she was stocked and ready for the first trip. Morgana christened her "The Owl Night Club" after all the late nights spent dreaming of her flights across the country. This was later shortened to "The Owl Club."

The Owl Club was coupled to the local engine line in Staten Island and rolled out south to Philadelphia once passengers had boarded and luggage had been loaded.

"As much as I enjoy being at sea, watching the land sprinkled with these little towns roll past is much more enjoyable to pass the time," Morgana explained.

"You cannot compare being on the open waters to this," Viktor said. "On the sea, there is fresh air. Here we are trapped in a box with the scent of flint and coal. On the *Ponthieva*, there was always something that needed to be done. We have been traveling half a day just sitting here."

"Well, I am enjoying every minute of it. If you are tired old man, the bed is in the next room," she said.

"Old man?" he questioned. "I am catching up on my reading."

She turned back to look out the window, knowing she could spark his passion with just a few choice words. "I also mentioned 'bed.'"

He was still unsure of how to handle such titillating comments from her. It had been years since they'd been intimate. Only in the last year had he noticed her body starting to change and become more womanly. It still seemed taboo to him to look at her that way, but he couldn't help it. She was beautiful. He loved her.

The Owl Club changed to another engine line in Philadelphia and started west. Farms rolled past the window as the rhythm of the track and the chug of the engine began to melt into the background as a soothing sound. The spring harvest was still a few weeks away as the cold nights lingered. Cows would blink their eyes at the young Morgana while they grazed in the nearly green grass. The forests were so thick that hardly a ray of light passed through the canopy. It was an amazing sight that played out in front of her—things so familiar yet different enough to capture her imagination.

Coffee and sandwiches were served to tide them over until supper. It was nice to have fewer people hovering about in their life. Elsie Smith was one of the two who was traveling with them. She was a good cook, had been with Morgana since she was a baby, and kept a private life.

Alaric Bichel had proved to be the most loyal and keen of the former Pinkerton guards that had been hired. He volunteered to join the Eriksons on the trip. One of the things Viktor liked most about Bichel was that he was not a big man. Instead, he was someone who could blend in with a gathering and observe. Bichel also liked to think in advance. Conversations with him were just that, conversations, not commands or one taking orders. Instead, he would ask questions and engage Morgana and Viktor in what they would like to do, what they might want to consider.

The four rolled on into the evening, watching the lamplights fill the streets of the towns where they stopped.

Morgana was the first to say it. "Each town we stop in has a station, a general store, and a saloon. Is this all we will see on our adventure?"

The Eriksons retired to the bedroom located at the front of the car, away from the living area, kitchen, and private bunks for Bichel and Smith in the back.

While getting accustomed to the sway of the car and the clatter of the wheels on the rails, Morgana asked Viktor the question they had both wanted to discuss. "Why won't you touch me, Viktor?"

"I want to touch you, Morgana. Really I do."

"Then touch me." She took his hand and moved it to her body. It felt good to have his hands on her.

"I . . . you . . . you look so young, Morgana," he finally said. His hand halted at her waist.

"Too young?"

"I love you, Morgana, I truly do. Still, there is something in me that sees your body and thinks it's—"

"Wrong?"

"I was going to say 'inappropriate.'"

"Oh, Viktor, you don't know. I have this feeling in me, this hunger that needs to be fed. I may look young to you, but I have desires building deep within me that only you can satisfy."

"I know."

"Do you? When you crawled into my bed that night, when you felt that need, I knew your body was too young, but I didn't say no. I didn't hold back. Please, Viktor."

He smiled and understood. They began to kiss. His hand again explored the areas of her body she liked best. The old pattern of pleasure quickly returned as if they had not waited fourteen years for this. Slowly, he began to enter her when she called out in pain. It brought him to a sudden stop with concern. "Are you all right?" he asked.

"I . . . I don't know what it is," she replied. "Try again." As he slowly worked forward, the pain she experienced was tremendous. Her nails dug into the skin of his back, and she yelped like an injured animal. "Don't stop. Push through. My body must have . . ." While she could not say it, they both knew of the returned virginal state she was in.

Breakfast the next morning was estranged for Smith and Bichel as the two lovers cooed in conversation. By afternoon, Smith and Bichel had found the evidence in cleaning. Neither said a word. Both told themselves that this mystery of their relationship might be solved one day.

Chapter Fifteen: Yellowstone

Year 1885
Viktor age 35
Morgana age 14

THE OWL CLUB decoupled at Livingston Station in Montana for the duration of their stay. From the window, Morgana could see the mysterious morning mist rising from the Yellowstone River. Snow capped the distant mountaintops even in midsummer. The world of wonder had been delivered to her window.

For fun, she slipped out of bed, not waking Viktor, put her favorite cylinder on the Edison, placed the needle down gently, and watched him jump from the bed to Gilbert and Sullivan's rousing "Behold the Lord High Executioner."

"The stage up to the park leaves in an hour," Bichel said loudly, entering the back door. "We all need to be up and ready for a full day."

The smile on the happy little girl running around the train, the loud music, and the dower look from Smith told Bichel all he needed to know when entering the car: Viktor was awake now.

Most of the mud from spring had dried, but there was enough below the dry surface to make the stage ride to camp take most of the day. On arrival to the initial camp site, they were overjoyed to see the eight large white canvas tents on raised wooden platforms.

"I'm just happy to be off that coach," Morgana said. She took a long stretch and rubbed her legs to improve the circulation from sitting so long in one place.

"Howdy." A man approached. He wore a thick dark mustache on tanned and darkened skin. His hat was wide in rim, turned up in front to keep weather off his face and let it roll down his back. Still in chaps and gloves, he extended his hand. "I'm Thatch," he said.

"Viktor Erikson."

"I'll be your guide and host while you're with us, Mr. Erikson."

"Please call me Viktor."

"Yes, Viktor, can do," Thatch replied.

"This is Morgana, Ms. Elsie Smith, and my personal agent, Mr. Alaric Bichel."

Thatch shook hands and tipped his hat for each introduction. "Pleasure to meet you all." He looked up to the sky. "Getting kind of late in the day for a ride, so let's have you folks settle, eat dinner, enjoy good night in the fresh air, and start first thing. Sound good?"

"It sounds delightful," Morgana said.

Viktor noticed the look in Morgana's eyes. It was the same look she'd had when they first met in Savannah. Thatch reminded Viktor of himself from those younger days. He looked to be a young man who had heeded the call to go west. The embodiment of a call for Manifest Destiny some thirty-five years prior, he looked wily and rugged from the miles, still a tenderfoot for the years.

Settling into camp after the ride, they cleaned the dust and mud from the trunks before opening them. Viktor wore pants, Morgana a riding dress. Both had a few layers of undergarments with shirts on top. Viktor looked smart with a large kerchief wrapped around his neck and tucked into the neck of his jacket.

Dinner was provided on tin plates around the campfire. They enjoyed a hearty amount of pork, beans, and some local bread that sopped up anything one couldn't scoop off with a fork.

"Tomorrow you will stand amongst the wonders of the Lord and see," Thatch explained. "You will feel small and helpless next to them and will ask yourself one question." He paused and made eye contact with each in the circle until coming to Viktor.

"What? What question?" Viktor blurted out.

"Why?" Thatch smiled. "Why did I spend so much time living this way when I could have been here?" Thatch smiled in reply to Viktor's stern and salty face.

"I think I understand," Viktor said. "I felt the same at sea long ago."

"You sailed, Mr. Erikson?" Smith asked.

"I did. It was once my life," he replied.

"Tomorrow will be a long day," Thatch said, collecting empty tins. "We are going to do a fair amount of riding over the next few days. Going to see some waterfalls and the lake before heading west to see the geysers."

"Geysers?" Morgana perked up.

"Yes, little lady, natural water fountains that shoot up from the ground."

"I am not so young, Mr. Thatch."

"It's just Thatch, ma'am," he said. "So, pack when you wake and be ready to ride. You get to keep what you carry. Each night you will find that camp was set by one of my team. They ride a day ahead of us so things are set and right when we get there. There is a guide a two days behind us with a group. If we fall behind, they will catch up. Yellowstone is too big to go alone. So we run this train. Any questions?"

The four looked excited enough to leave that moment for the next day's adventure but didn't say a word.

"Well," Thatch said, "best we get a good night's rest before the sunrise."

The first day introduced them to the amazing sites Thatch had described: large trees, big valleys, deep ravines, and the wonders of nature. It was difficult to believe that anything could be more spectacular than that first day.

On the second day, the group had again risen early, packed, and ridden southeast. This pattern was repeated over the next several days with rewarding vistas over towering peaks, lower and upper falls, and a deep night's sleep.

After turning south along the river, the talk around the fire each night contained stories about mud fountains, bubbling pits and cauldrons, birds, bears, and wildflowers that would inspire a lifetime's work for any great artist.

On occasion, Thatch would hold up his hand, which both stopped the party cold and silenced anyone talking. Quick with his rifle when needed, he explained about the massive moose and immense buffalos he'd caught a glimpse of in the distance. "I much rather let 'em pass by."

At night, Thatch would tell stories about the lost of Yellowstone. There were tales of those who had gotten separated from their party never to be found. Many stories he told focused on the great suffering people endured to survive. Then there were stories about Indians—the Sheepeaters, Shoshone, and the Bannock—in the area who had lived on and loved this land for generations.

It happened one night, about two days' ride south of the main camp where they had all first met, during one of Thatches tales about the park that a man stepped out from the woods and quietly approached the fire. Thatch was the first to notice him and instructed the others to stay calm. The man had dark, long, wild hair. What he wore looked to be the color of hide and very warm. When Thatch offered the man his plate of food, he took it, his high cheekbones protruding from his face with a look of emaciation. The man nodded his head and began to eat as much as he could. Joining the group, he sat at the fire to enjoy the dish. When the man had finished, Viktor offered him his plate as well. The man hesitated at first but took it in the end. It, too, was quickly eaten. Thatch walked over to his pack, pulled out a cloth bag of dried meats and jarred fruits, and handed the bag to the man. He inspected the fabric and the wax paper that wrapped the dried goods, smelling deeply and closing his eyes to savor with what seemed delight. Rested and full, the man stood and said one word before silently slipping back into the wilderness: "eh-shun."

——⋗●⋖——

These weeks in the park seemed like a new life. Not only was this time reminiscent of the adventures he had loved in his first life on the sea, but it was also refreshing to see the wilderness bare and unmolested by the footprints of industry. Viktor could feel a longing returning. If it was for the sea, it was for exploration, a life of bold ventures where his life was his own to master. The sentiment stirred him awake the night before their planned coach ride back to Livingston. In the morning, they would meet the coach and return to the train car.

Outside his tent, the moon was nearly full and filled the valley with an enchanting glow. Sounds of the night moved through the trees with a cool mountain breeze. He could see the clearing ahead where the food locker hung in the trees from man and beast. Still, he had a slight craving he could not fill and thought a bit of food might do.

Inspecting the rope that held the locker up—nearly ready to give up on the complicated knot the back woodsman had tied and no sailor would ever fumble—he heard voices in the distance. Viktor stepped closer to the source of the conversation. He stopped in his tracks when he realized it was Morgana and Thatch. The two were wrapped in a blanket. Under the moonlight, he could see the bright white skin that had been protected from the sun as the two lovers, naked, were in engaged in the physical entanglements of the flesh.

Both fulfilled, the conversation they held revealed to Viktor that Morgana did not want to leave Thatch but felt she must. It had been delightful and romantic, but it was a short dream that they would need to awake from soon.

Thatch was trying to sway her to stay a little bit longer. He talked about plans, long term and short. Everything they would need was in Livingston or in the park. She could be his lover, a great mother, and his wife.

Those words, "mother" and "wife," were lost on Morgana. Viktor could hear in her voice the same exasperated tones, defending her dislike for children, babies, and being treated as someone's property. Thatch had no idea of the true nature of the situation.

Viktor was hurt. He had suspected some interest between the two but not action, not this certainty. And this seemed so very real, the pain in his heart, like a shard torn through flesh. To see her under this boy gnarled at the trust he once had in Morgana. Viktor felt small, as if he were only a wisp of a shadow compared to this brilliant light of youth. His feelings twisted from lowered confidence and betrayal to pain that quickly boiled to anger.

"Morgana!" Viktor's voice bellowed in the darkness.

"Viktor?" She scrambled to her feet, wrapping the blanket around her, while Thatch grabbed his pants and slipped them on. "Viktor," she said again in panic. "Don't come over here."

"I won't," he said simply. "When you are done, we will need to talk."

Morgana joined Viktor by the last glowing embers from that night's fire. The stick in his hand poked at the white ash. Water that had been poured over the pit to extinguish the blaze had missed most of its target, leaving a gray mush outline next to the partially glowing coals.

"Viktor," Morgana said in a low voice, "how much did you witness?"

"Does it matter? Enough. Enough to know what has been going on this trip. Enough to realize that I am too old for you. You must see me as some colossal, old, and cripple man past his prime."

"No, I don't see you that way."

He looked up from the scratching in the dirt. "This hurts me, Morgana. I've had suspicions in the past, but to be confronted with them like this? I have to wonder where our trust has gone. "

"We both have water with us. I have seen that vile you carry for emergencies. I know I have a similar one."

"Wait, your first thought here is to go straight for the water?" he asked.

"Yes, obviously. What did you have in mind? What did you think we could do? Just walk away?"

"I thought that things between us were over, that you wanted a better partner, that we needed to make other plans or arrangements. It is obvious you no longer love me."

"Love you? Of course I love you, poor Viktor. He was just . . . an amusement."

"Being with him was fun? That is why you were with him, for fun? And I am no longer fun?"

"I did not say that. You are fun, just a different type of fun," she explained.

Viktor took a moment to think about the implications. For generations, men had been to whore houses away from a spouse, looking to have fun and fulfill their needs. How was this different for Morgana? How would this be different for any woman? They must have similar needs, similar passions that needed attention. To think otherwise would have been naïve. Still, thinking through this didn't hurt any less. He had spent decades with her. His life was an investment in the two of them together.

"What is your plan?" Viktor finally asked.

"Thatch, well, he we would have to."

"And?"

"Well, how much do we really need Ms. Smith and Mr. Bichel?"

"Curse you, Morgana. Curse you for even thinking this. They are trusted, loyal. I have grown very fond of Mr. Bichel, and I have seen you with Smith—she treats you like she would her own."

"The best of this," she continued without consideration of a word he said, "is that they will all get a second chance at life. They will be able to see this wonderful park for a whole other lifetime."

"No, please no," Viktor said to her. "I cannot believe how little you care for others. How you toy with people. How you burn your boat before you have landed."

"It is a simple matter of logic, what we need, and how to get it."

"You could just break his heart and tell him it was for one night. Leave him behind. That is what normal people do. Just break his heart—don't destroy his life."

He could see her stubborn expression under the moon. She looked angry in a way he was unfamiliar with. "Very well," she said. "In the morning, we will rise like nothing happened, take the coach into town, and head home."

"Good. Thank you."

"And these two flibbertigibbets will spread gossip to the rest of the house staff, undermine our authority on our own grounds, and start rumors that detail falsehoods of our lives."

He waited for her to finish. "This water you want to give them, it is to prevent gossip?"

"More than that. It's to sustain our place in the world."

"I am going to go to bed, Morgana," he said. Viktor turned and walked to his tent. Removing his nightshirt and getting under the covers, he warmed but never returned to that blissful place he'd left. Gone were the glorious memories of the adventure. Distant were the thoughts of freedom and a longing to return to his life on the sea.

⸻ ◆ ⸻

In the morning, he woke late. There were no early stirrings of packing, no clatters of morning coffee and breakfast being made, just the peaceful sounds of nature that filled the air. In the hopes that last night was only sleep filled with nightmares, Viktor closed his eyes again. He stayed in this warm cocoon of bedding until he heard the first cry of a baby. He then knew with certainty it was no nightmare, no dream, but the reality of knowing a strong-willed woman named Morgana.

It was late in the evening before Viktor finally said something to Morgana. She had teased and pleaded with him since he'd left the tent that morning to talk to her, reply to what she said, and pay attention to her. The train car jerked on a lose spike, and the jarring movement forced him to look up and lock eyes with her.

"Don't be so angry, Viktor. You have what you want still. You have me. You have the gold. What more is there? So what if there are a few indiscretions?

Who does it hurt? A few drops of water and all these problems disappear," she said coldly. "You should just be thankful I haven't done this to you."

The thought sent a chill through him. "You would do that to me? What happened to the trust? What about the plan to be with each other the rest of our lives?"

"We will. This is the plan. We are living it."

"But not exclusively."

"Oh, poor Viktor," she said with a pouted lip. "Are you suggesting that you stayed true to me on those trips to the city? All of them?"

"I did," he replied. "Didn't you? You told me that Boston was about business, Manhattan was about business."

Her look was flat and unchanged. It told him the truth of the moment: there were others.

"I'm not sure what is to be done here," Viktor said, settling into his chair. "I don't think I can trust you to pour me another drop to drink for fear you may find another to your liking."

"You carry the water, don't you?" she asked.

"I have a few drops with me, just in case."

"In case of what?"

"In case you or I were injured. In the event that things might be hopeless and we're in need of a way out." His voice was more distant, reflective to a more innocent time. "When we have taken the water, we've had our baby teeth and struggled with teething. I came to the conclusion that with this water, we are nearly reborn, unharmed, pure in a state where we are whole again." He looked out the window at the rolling landside. "If you were thrown from a horse, trampled—there are so many ways to lose you in our adventures—I could bring you back."

"That is so sweet to think of my well-being," Morgana said. She moved to his side and took his arm. Sweetly, she said into his ear, "You mean so much to me, Viktor. The others were just pleasures of the flesh. You have my heart. You always will."

"There will be questions," he said.

"We will come up with answers, just like with that general at Fort Brooke."

He looked at her with the stern face of a father. "What did you do with the babies?"

"The Shoshone man returned last night after you went to bed."

"The Indian?"

"Yes, the one we gave food to. He had apparently been following us, hoping to find more food. He was traveling with his family. They all looked so hungry, so I gave them the rest of our supplies."

"You are such a philanthropist," he said sarcastically. "What happened to the babies?"

"Are you not listening? I gave the Shoshone the food and the three babies. He was with his family. They will take care of them, treat them like their own."

All Viktor could do was shake his head in disbelief at what she described. "That doesn't make it right. He will raise those three as Shoshone. It will be a very hard life for them. Why do you think they look so emaciated? You may have given them a second life, but it will not be an easy one."

"Balderdash. Hardship builds character."

"The coach driver did not believe your story that they were lost. Thatch isn't the kind of man to get lost. I can hear the coachman's words still," he told her. "We were fortunate he took us back to Livingston. Sometimes I want to just slap some sense into you, Morgana. What if they return like the crew of the *Ponthieva*? You are planting seeds of hatred for our future. We will have to be even more cautious."

"Luck will always smile on us, my love, as long as we are together."

Alone, the two traveled into the night on The Owl Club, heading east, returning home.

∞ 22 ∞

Stretching

Year 2053
Olivia age 25

O LIVIA NEEDED TO take a few minutes and asked the floor nurse to watch Viktor while she grabbed coffee. The cafeteria in this hospital was very comfortable. It reminded her of a high-end restaurant in some sections. Other areas were designed as work spaces. Some spots looked like a coffee house. There were areas to grieve, locations for families to converse and catch up, even little nooks in the corners where you could tuck away and do a little reading during a summer shower. The designers of this cafeteria had several different types of people in mind.

Walking back with her coffee in hand, she noticed a wall with a series of names and photos. These were a frequent sighting in many hospitals to recognize the history or thank donors. Her hot coffee cooling, she began to scan the wall. In this incarnation of the hospital, they had taken many of the older photos and history to share the story of St. John's purpose and goals. "Committed to the Progress of Medicine" was in large font. "Thank you to all who helped us reach our goals!" was below it. The black and white images capturing the ghosts who once worked on these grounds started the story on the left. They stood in front of stone buildings on sunny days, motionless for the slow shutter to capture the moment. Moving right along the walls, the grain of the images began to improve. Bright outdoor photos that leveraged the natural maximum sunlight moved to photos inside the halls of the hospital with a powerful flash. Sharp lines of black and white followed to show the new facilities with shovels ready for the groundbreaking. Brick and mortar buildings were then replaced by color photos of poured concrete into shaped columns. People standing with patients were replaced by machines holding the sick on beds for examination. Farther right, she began to recognize images that would have been from her lifetime in the old high definition all the way to the current hospital in the holographic snippets of movement and interaction.

She returned her focus to the far left while stretching her back. There was a small audible "pop" as she turned and her back aligned from sitting all that time. Bending a little to the front to repeat part of her yoga warm up she did each day, her face came close to a photo she didn't notice previously. It was lower on the wall, black and white, very grainy, and she recognized the face. "Viktor?" The image was marked 1948.

"One hundred and five years ago?" she said. With her free hand, she placed her palm over the part of the face currently bandaged on Viktor. "It could be him, but it's not the best photo," she said to herself. "I only have one eye and half a face to go on." It might be him, the same basic frame with a similar shape of the face, but one could not be certain about these things.

A few minutes later, Olivia returned to Viktor and thanked the floor nurse for her time. There was no change in his condition. It looked like he had not moved during her time away, still wrapped in the white layers of blankets and sheets tucked into his bed.

"Viktor," she said alone in the room with him, "how old are you?"

His eye closed, the only movement was the slow rise and fall from his breathing.

"What secrets do you have?"

There was no reply. Olivia decided to keep reading to him to pass the time.

Chapter Sixteen: Chicago

Year 1893
Viktor age 43
Morgana age 22

THE TABULATED CHART that had originally won his heart sat on his bedside table. He had grown tired of looking at the ages both he and Morgana would be most compatible. The charts clearly indicated that there were times the two could be lovers and other ages when the responsibility would be for the elder to keep safe the younger before the water was consumed and the process started for the other. Both were in the prime of the nearly thirty-year life span when the two would be aligned, yet it had been nearly two years since he had actually laid eyes on Morgana.

He remembered the moment she left very clearly. How she promised it would only be a fortnight in the city to support the cause. "The cause" was a code he understood to be part of her life he was not to share. Just as he had been a part of a men's club, this was only for her.

At first, she had left for Manhattan to join the newly formed National American Women's Suffrage Association, which was made by several of the women she had supported a lifetime earlier. The unification of two groups, the National Suffrage Association and the American Woman Suffrage Association, was ideal for Morgana. She no longer had to choose one group or the other. Instead, she put her full attention to the combined efforts. There were notes and letters at first, but the days between arrivals became longer. When last she wrote it was from Chicago, praising the work of her friend Susan B. Anthony.

The fears from Yellowstone still haunted Viktor. The staff members at the estate were vetted regularly. Additional guards were hired. This sense of scrutiny and inspection had turned the staff sour from the goodwill invested for holidays and paid leave prior to the trip out west. Some left on their own, others he replaced for the smallest infraction or suspicion.

Many weeks would pass when Viktor would sit alone behind the safety of the walls. He spent days in the vault with his treasures, organizing and accounting for each piece. On occasion, he would meet with carpenters to discuss ideas on building what he would call "safety mechanisms" to prevent the ability to find a hypothetical room or ways to provide additional protection.

In the summer of 1893, a telegram arrived informing Viktor that Morgana was injured and hospitalized in Chicago. By day's end, he had contacted the rail yard to prep The Owl Club and it was connected to the next train heading west. By the next night, Viktor sat by Morgana's side.

"What happened?" he asked the woman in the room.

"She was speaking at the Women's Pavilion at the fair, and one of the members of the audience didn't like what she said about her rights and threw a brick."

Outside the edge of the wrapping around her face, he could see the darkened bruises. "Will she recover?"

"Nearly lost an eye, but the doctor says she should recover. Are you her father?"

Viktor took a moment before turning to answer. "Yes. And you are?"

"My name is Alice. I am good friends with your daughter. We have been traveling together trying to recruit new members to our organization. Do you support her in these efforts?"

He turned back to Morgana. "I do. She is my everything, and I support her fully."

"That is wonderful to hear. We need more active registered voters to support our efforts," Alice said.

"Viktor?" Morgana mumbled.

"Yes, dear, I am here."

"Oh, Viktor, it is so good to see you."

"I got the wire and came right away. How do you feel?"

"It hurts," she moaned. "I can't bear to have the window open. All I want to do is sleep." She winced trying to move.

"There, there, don't move. I will find the doctor."

"No, wait, Viktor, don't go yet. I've missed you so much these last years. I should have come home to see you. I have so many things to tell you."

"It is all right. You are safe here."

"I love you, Viktor. It has been too long. Kiss me. Kiss me before you go again."

Viktor looked to Alice and then kissed Morgana on the cheek.

"Has it been that long? Kiss me like you used to," she said.

"Morgana, your friend Alice is here with us. You remember Alice?"

"Yes, of course. Thank you for staying with me, Alice."

"Your father was just telling me how much he supports our cause."

"Yes. My father," Morgana said. He could hear the disappointment in her voice. She added, "We can catch up later, Father. Go find the doctor."

The word from the doctor was similarly dour to what Alice had reported. Morgana had nearly lost her right eye and may not regain full sight. There would be a large scar under the bandages as the doctor had tied the two flaps of skin together with twenty-two surgical sutures made of iodized catgut. She was also suffering from spells that suggested some type of contusion to the brain.

Upon returning to the room, he found that Morgana had fallen back to sleep. Alice remained with her in the darkness, holding her hand and soothing her with kind words and an unfamiliar tune about their cause.

"The two of you are close?" he asked.

"Very close. We are more than friends," Alice replied. "Closer than sisters."

"I'm glad to hear this. It has been some time since we have spoken, and it is encouraging to know she has not been alone," he explained.

"I would be lost without her," she said.

"Alice, do you have a last name?"

Her voice was hard in reply. "I do not have a last name. I will not carry the name of the man who calls himself father nor will I take a man's name in wedlock."

"So I will just call you Alice?"

"Yes, that is best."

The Owl Club jerked when the wheels of the locomotive first started to rotate and grab traction before the initial skid of forward motion. Viktor, in his usual chair, settled in for the journey. Alice found her place in the living area chair while Morgana, half curled up on the floor at Alice's feet, looked into her handheld mirror.

Morgana tried to move her jaw under the bandage. She could feel the tight restraint from the sutures. Her finger began to tickle at the edge of the wrap around her head, and it loosened a bit where it was most taut.

"Don't pick at it. It will come undone," Alice said.

"I must look like a mummy," Morgana replied. "I certainly feel like one with my face swaddled."

"Leave it be," Alice reminded.

Morgana could not resist the urge to play with it, to see it. She wanted to touch the wound and understand the full devastation that man with a brick and filled with anger had caused. The loose end was quickly undone, and the bandage that circumvented her head quickly unfurled.

"Morgana! What have you done?" Alice said.

"Leave her be," Viktor said. "She needs to know."

Viktor shrunk deep into his lounge chair from the sinister stare Alice shot at him. "Never presume you can command me, Viktor," Alice warned. And in the time it took for Alice to reveal her place, the long bandage lay undone on the floor at her feet.

The reflection in Morgana's handheld looking glass was spellbinding. The deep cut of flesh bound together with dark twine was enveloped in the deep sea of purples, browns, and yellows of bruised skin. Her eye was partially closed and forced Morgana to turn her head at an irregular angle for her good eye to reflect the horror.

The train took full speed around the bottom of Lake Michigan and headed east for the estate across the flatlands of Indiana and Ohio. Viktor had already wired ahead to have his man inquire about the best doctors in Manhattan.

It was somewhere west of the Allegheny River that Morgana spoke again. "You know, there are all types of fountains, Alice."

It caught Viktor's attention from the book in hand.

"There are?" said Alice.

"There was that beautiful fountain in Chicago. It was so detailed in design. And when the wind would blow just right, those unsuspecting souls would get wet from the spray," Morgana said.

"I remember that morning well when we sat by it watching," Alice replied.

"Viktor, do you remember that fountain we saw in Yellowstone?"

"How could I forget?" he said.

"It would blast its spout hundreds of feet in the air with a hot spray like a warm summer shower."

"That was a great day, Morgana."

"There is another fountain we've found, Viktor and I," Morgana said to Alice.

The plea softly fell from his lips. "Please don't."

"Oh, Viktor, I love Alice. I love Alice like I love you. It does not mean I love you any less or her any more—it's just a different love. There is enough love for us to share. She needs to know about us. She needs to be part of us, part of our plans."

"Morgana, you have been looking at your reflection for hours like Narcissus at the springs. Please, I beg you, think about what you are doing. Do not drown in this moment caught in your own reflection."

When she turned away from her mirror and their eyes met, he knew. He could see the same look she had given him over the years when he believed her heart was his and his alone. His slight nod of the head turned into an audible acceptance. "Morgana, you tear my heart apart as if it were warm bread in your fingers." Exhausted from the emotional ringer she had twisted him over for so many years, he said, "If you really love her, then tell her. I trust you. I trust you with my life."

<hr/>

When the train arrived at the station, his carriage and driver were there to greet them. Viktor introduced his driver to Alice, the new nanny of his adopted child, Morgana. She was a beautiful baby: raven hair, putty skin, bright eyes, and a glowing smile.

Chapter Seventeen: Dining Room

Year 1913
Viktor age 62
Morgana age 20

ALICE HAD BEEN a committed nurse to baby Morgana over the years. Viktor appreciated that very little effort was called on him to raise her again. Alice, along with three nursemaids, could meet any fancy the child might have after the events of Chicago. Alice and Morgana were inseparable like sisters over the years, bedding together at night, tootling around the grounds on any leisurely afternoon, and singing tunes over breakfast. They were good years for Morgana, another chance at another privileged life.

Morgana was now older in physical age than when she and Viktor originally met. Viktor felt left out of her life. By this time in the life plan, Viktor should have taken the water again, Morgana should be the elder, and the two should be sharing in the bliss and rapture of each other's companionship. Instead, Viktor had become an outsider. He was a guest in his own home as decisions were made without so much a notice or consolation.

His love was now talking about sharing the prize of this water with her new companion.

Viktor had given up insisting that they have at least one meal together. He missed seeing Morgana each day. She went missing for weeks with Alice and would return on a whim. On the few occasions when they might have breakfast, he discovered the two kept very busy schedules. There were meetings to attend. Meetings would plan for rallies. Rallies would recruit more members. More members led to additional meetings. Once Morgana turned old enough to travel, it was as if she had disappeared. The Owl Club made regular trips to Manhattan, Boston, and Washington. All the planning and travel cost money, but no one wanted to include Viktor's name as a donor, especially him. These activities needed to be under the anonymity of a wealthy supporter to the movement. The Owl Club was now only a name *he* used as the train car carried a fresh coat of paint to cover the true name and symbols marking its ownership. It now wore a sash. It now carried slogans of the movement.

Viktor felt numb when the telegraph wire arrived at the door from the Pennsylvania Railroad Company on that summer day of 1913:

PRIVATE TRAIN CAR THE NIGHT OWL CLUB VANDALIZED. BURNED REMAINS IN POTOMAC RAIL YARD. NO INJURIES REPORTED. PLEASE ADVISE.

"It was only a thing," he said to himself. "I am feeling my age." Viktor took to his study and telephoned the operator for a direct connection to his legal team in Manhattan. He informed the other line of the telegraph wire and the train car. This conversation then changed into the rewriting of all the documentation supporting his ownership of the estate and property. Viktor was through with this game Alice and Morgana had been playing. Viktor would take control if the two would not participate in the plans they had made.

All the accounts in joint, lines of credit that had shared their name, and outstanding bills were to be paid in full and closed. New lines in his name alone were to be opened. Instructions to the staff and guards were clear: Alice and Morgana were to be considered trespassers. If they thought of him as a strict and overbearing father, he would treat them as if he were one.

His driver and personal guard drove him in the Oldsmobile into Manhattan by the week's end. They were followed closely by a second car with four additional men from his security detail. Recently, Viktor had begun to think he might be too cautious. His mind would think back to the chances taken on the *Ponthieva*, his time of adventure with Morgana, nearly losing his life to the men he once trusted, and the incident at Yellowstone. If there was one thing he had learned over the many years it was that revenge builds into action, and he must prevent those actions to keep his life.

His lawyers guided him to sign several documents after review. They informed him that Alice and Morgana had already called several times inquiring as to what had happened and why there were sudden changes. As instructed, the two were told to contact Viktor directly for details. He was pleased. His heart had been led astray for decades. He thought that he had loved Morgana, that their story was so special and unique no one else could ever know him in the same way. But she had taken advantage of his good nature. She was to blame for this series of changes having ignored him, having broken the pact, for putting herself in the situation where she would be reborn twice while he aged, hidden in the safety of this stony tomb at the estate. She would continue her life with new adventures, find new love, and change the world while he would be forgotten and rot. He still had power. He still had control. He was still in command, and he would demonstrate that, if need be, to get her back or to gain her attention.

There had not been a time of certain security since safes and locks could be picked or broken in the 1850s. Even with every effort Viktor made to safeguard the gold and riches on the estate, he had not achieved much more than digging a hole in the ground and surrounding it with measures of safety. It was once true that the distance to the estate allowed for anonymity, but surrounding parcels to the estate had been developed and he eventually had neighbors. The *Ponthieva* was once his planned escape route, but an escape by sea was no longer an option. He needed to find a new way to keep the things he owned from others. He needed to maintain his wealth and value without intervention from the eyes of the growing governmental control with the Sixteenth Amendment.

Under his instruction and the guidance of the legal minds of this small firm, a bank was identified in Manhattan where a private vault under armed guard could keep a volume of precious metals and gems. The safety deposit box would be a vault that only he was allowed access to, and several key identifiers would be needed to gain entry. The materials in the vault were unlike cash, which was open to the auditing of a federal or state agency. Properties hidden in this box would go unnoticed for what he hoped would be centuries. No interest accrued, but no penalties applied. This treasure would sit no better than the top of the pyramid from where they came, undisturbed.

Two of his oldest and most senior trusted staff entered the hidden room on the estate following this meeting with the legal team. They spent the following two weeks creating and boxing everything in the room that had been collected decades earlier, starting with the bars and ending with loose coins. Cash and banknotes would be the only valuables that Viktor kept on the property in an undisclosed location.

After the job was complete, the next step in his plan proceeded. Under the guise of broken sewage pipes in the Manhattan bank, Viktor oversaw the transfer of all the crates from the estate by trucks marked with the name of a construction company to the basement-level private vault. The glow of the room was extinguished. The fear of robbery and larceny was now gone. Only workers knew of the wooden boxes filling an impenetrable vault, and the two top men on his team were rewarded with private homes and full bank accounts of their choosing to live out the remainder of their only life.

Sleeping soundly for the first time since Yellowstone, Viktor woke at the sound of a single shot. He leapt from the bed and dressed quickly, finding his newest sidearm in his bedside drawer. With the gun loaded and fully cocked, he waited for a call of "all clear" before exiting his room.

At the bottom of the stairwell on the main floor, he saw in an instant an image that filled his heart with both regret and accomplishment: Morgana had returned to him. In the darkness of night, she had found a way back into his home and heart with Alice. She now cried over the body of her love in grief, her sorrow filling the halls of the mansion with wails.

"The water!" she cried out when she saw him. "Viktor, get the water—quickly!"

He traversed down the stairs slowly to the growing pool of blood on the cold marble floor. Three of his guards watched as there was little to do in the moment.

"The water, Viktor, the water." She broke down.

"There is nothing for her here."

"You monster," she said. Morgana rose from her fallen love to meet the man she blamed eye to eye. "You are going to allow her to die at your front door?"

Looking down at the body and back up, he said, "She is already dead. You killed her by bringing her here, by bringing her into our lives. You knew the rules. You drafted them by chart and scale and sold them to me by lies of your heart of love immortal. The blame is at your feet." Viktor turned to his men. "Please call the local police and wake the cleaning staff. We will need to clean up this mess."

Morgana, in a rage, broke from the moment and dashed down the hall to the library. The mantel which once glowed with the magical elixir was now empty. She pulled on the book to unlock the hidden door and forced it to open faster, but she found an empty room. On the shelf, she pushed the small button that once opened the hidden vault lined with gold and glittering treasure, the results of her bold ventures. But the room was barren, a feeling that now matched her soul.

"It's over," Viktor said, his calm and even voice nearly sinister. "Your tournaments played on my heart with other sports have ended. There is no prize here for you, no treasure, no trophy."

"Why, Viktor? Why would you cut us off? Abandon us in the middle of our good works? Have orders to shoot to kill intruders?"

"You left me, Morgana, you left me for another love. We were supposed to be together forever; that was the plan."

"Is that really what you want, Viktor?"

"It was."

"Was?"

"Morgana, there is no place for you here. You have made your choice. I am getting old and will need to find a new person to care and raise me. You have already shown I can no longer charge you with that responsibility. You abhor the idea of raising babies, something you have repeated to me time and again."

Leaving the vault, exiting the library, and slowly making her way down the corridor to where the body of her dead love lay, Morgana seemed physically in pain from the shock. "Just give me my share," she said in a loud, clear voice.

"You've forfeited your share," Viktor replied.

She turned back and ran to him. Her arms wrapped under the robe and clutched tightly to his side. "You can't do this. I have nothing, nothing."

Her pleas did not prompt pity or remorse. Instead, with her arms locked around him and staff attending to the body down the hall, he felt remorse. "Perhaps I have been too hard," Viktor said.

Alice's last name turned out to be Humphries. She had been a runaway from Meriwether, Georgia, at the age of fifteen. Her father had abused and beaten Alice. She had no siblings, and no living relatives could be found. Her criminal record and series of arrests in several cities were easy to discover. Local police believed that she had been robbing the estate and the action from the guards was justifiable.

Viktor began to soften in proximity to Morgana. He agreed to bury Alice in a private plot on the estate. An extensive list of suffragettes attended and paid expenses to join in a private service. Viktor kept his distance from the day, respecting that the only true family Alice had known were the fellow members of the rights movement she deeply believed in. He only asked that there was no mention of his name as a matter of anonymity for support. This was something that the women could understand now that they knew there was some type of connection between him, Alice, and Morgana during those years.

⤖

There were no rules or expectations as Viktor drank the water again. Everything was in his name. The treasures and remaining water were locked in locations only he knew. Morgana would stay in the small cottage on the estate that overlooked the bay off to the Atlantic. It was not as extravagant as the main house but not nearly as sparse as she sometimes complained.

A trio of trusted consultants were to look after Viktor and his interests for four years. One was a nanny he had provided careful instructions to as his elder self. Another was chief counsel at the small law firm of which he was the only client. Finally, there was his personal guard. Outside of daily interests and activities, the three would have to agree unanimously on any business to be done.

This produced a very peaceful time. The staff was paid regularly, holidays were given, the grounds were kept, maintenance continued, and interest compounded regularly with low yield on the cash and savings. Nothing was bought or sold. No drama carried out on the cold marble floors.

It occurred to Viktor in the summer of 1920 that he had not celebrated his birthday in nearly four decades. Mentally, he was now somewhere close to one hundred years in age. Physically, he was a little boy, no more than six. Morgana was also close to one hundred years old, but by all outward appearances, she was an exquisite woman in her late twenties.

There had been recent days when Viktor would see Morgana walking the grounds outside his window and wonder what was on her mind. He could remember the passion, he could remember the feelings of love, but now he only knew the need for commitment. The only other stranger in this land of time and space was Morgana. The rest were barnacles that needed scraping. So, he invited her to a private dinner in the main house.

Comfortably seated in the cozy room, the two had little to say during a service of soup. The occasional clinking of glasses and tapping of spoons on the dishes seemed loud in the silence.

"It's good to see you again," she said.

"And to see you. How have you been these years?"

"Well, I have taken to reading, enjoying my solitude and reflection, living off my allowance."

He smiled, knowing that money would be one of many topics. He let it pass. "I asked for a cake to be made this evening."

"What is the cause for celebration?"

"I have come to realize that I am one hundred and four years old this year."

She nearly spilled her water at the thought. "You are? Well, congratulations to you."

"That would place you somewhere near a hundred or more."

"A lady never tells." She did not do the math but trusted his accuracy. "It's close. Still, I don't feel old."

"You certainly do not look it. You are as beautiful as the first day we met in Savannah."

She placed the napkin over her lips to cover the blush. "Thank you."

He thought for a moment, searching for another topic that might keep her engaged. "I read that Michigan ratified the amendment for the right to vote."

She smiled and nodded politely.

"All that hard work, all the time you spent," he added. "It made a difference."

Sadly, she looked at the table before her and said, "I wish I could have done more. I wish I could be there, in Washington."

The two sat in silence, not knowing what to say to one another.

Viktor finally broke the silence, saying, "There is something else I have come to know."

"And what is that?"

"We are our only best companions."

"How do you mean?"

"There is no one else who would ever understand what we have been through. No one else knows the times in which we have lived."

"That's true," she said.

"Did you find that comfort with Alice?"

Her fork dropped to her plate. "That is a name I have not heard or mentioned in years. I have tried to stop thinking about her."

"My apologies. I . . . I did not intend to hurt you. It was merely a curiosity. You see, the only person that I have spent time thinking about, longing for, or believing was my companion was, well, you. And you are here. You are someone I can still try to connect with. It is the reason I ask."

Morgana was silent as dinner was served. It was a succulent pheasant from the grounds, with carrots, potatoes, and Brussels sprouts that smelled delicious compared to the meals she had been taking in the guest house. She thought back to their first meal together, recalling that over the many lifetimes it had always been some type of bird with a side of starch and vegetable they had shared most frequently.

"Alice was not a companion who would talk about old times," she eventually replied. "She was not one to yarn about the past. The company we would keep was about passion for our cause, passion for one another. She made me feel something I had not known before with any other person."

Viktor began to sour from the conversation and now wished he had not started it.

"I can see that this is upsetting," she said, "but it should not be. It was nothing you were lacking, nothing you could have done differently. It was something greater between us than anything individually." She reflected again to a different time. "Do you remember your father?"

"I think I do. I remember images and moments, but I don't know that I remember *him*."

"I remember my father. He was kind and protective of me. He listened. There was nothing I could not tell him, nothing I could do that would change the way he felt about me. My time with Alice was similar to that time with my father: trust without question, a belief that she would be with me no matter what."

"And you do not feel that with me? Have never felt that with me?"

"No. No, I felt desire and a rush of pleasure. I felt safe in your arms from villains and criminals and knew you would catch me when I fell. But many times, I felt frustrated that we were not more intimate."

"But we . . ."

"Mentally intimate . . . comfortable with one another."

He dabbed at his lips with the napkin. "I see."

"Thank you for having me for dinner tonight. I was hoping that you and I could one day speak again, maybe even be friends again."

"I would like that. I would like that very much," he said. It was the most honest moment he could recall. "Now that we are friends over chicken, imagine how close we will be after cake."

She laughed. It was the first time she had laughed for some time. Knowing he could still make her laugh gave him hope and began to melt his hardened heart.

❧ 25 ❧

Chapter Eighteen: Harlem

Year 1923
Viktor age 9
Morgana age 31

IN THE FALL of 1923, Viktor made note to Morgana of General Wu on the cover of *Time* magazine on the newsstand they passed. Summer had not entirely left, and autumn was close to arriving. It made for a beautiful day in Manhattan.

Among the street cars, elevated trains, and cars, the two felt entirely safe in the cocoon their hired men provided. Eight armed guards kept pace with the two walking into Times Square. Everyday citizens stepped aside to clear a path for these serious men.

"We have to come back at night," Morgana said. "I would just love to see the bright lights at night."

"We will do just that then—come back tonight," Viktor said.

"We should find a speakeasy or go into Harlem and see live jazz. Wouldn't that be grand?" she asked.

"It would."

They entered the hotel a few blocks later and took the elevator to the eighth floor. Only three of the men joined them on the elevator while the rest took another.

Once settled in their room, Morgana spoke up. "Do you think we need all those men with us? All the time?"

"It's for our protection."

"I know, I know, but it seems so limiting to see the world from over the shoulders of such gorillas. Do you think we might find some shorter ones so that I can get a better view?"

"I only see you looking up at the buildings. Do you need a better view?" he asked.

"I would like to see some faces rather than the backsides of the same men."

"We can take fewer with us tonight to the jazz club, if you would like."

"Seven instead of all eight? No deal."

"Five," he bartered.

"Four," she said.

"Four it is. I'll let them know."

Harlem was jumping. The music in the shows was faster. "The Stride" blended the keys on the piano into a rhythm difficult to keep up with but raced the pulse of onlookers from the darkness to the staged piano under the lights. After the second act with "The Lion," the two skipped over to the next club to see Jelly Roll Morton with his New Orleans jazz, which was entirely different.

The cool night air felt good against the dizzying intoxication of hot music and strong drink. They decided to walk a few blocks with one of the men while the other three would get the car and catch up.

Nightlife along the streets was a play filled with characters. With each step, the scene would change and the story play on. There were desperate lovers arguing, dancers auditioning for the world with hats out and spare change accepted, and good folks on stoops enjoying the cool air.

When the Oldsmobile pulled up, Viktor and Morgana complied with the request to get in from their man.

"I think it's entirely foolish," she went on. "While I adore each and every one of you, having you all around is just too much."

"Morgana, please. We have them with us to make certain we are safe."

"Viktor, I am not sure if we are truly living if all we think of is prevention. There has to be a balance."

Down the streets from Harlem, the car crossed back into the city. Within a few blocks, they were back at the hotel, safe. One of the guards opened the door to the back, allowing Viktor and Morgana to disembark.

"The lights!" Morgana declared. "We were going to see the lights. Do you think they are still on?"

"Yes, yes, they are still on," he said.

She pulled at his arm. "Let's go, get a move on."

Viktor looked to the gaggle of men on his flank. They shared expressions of being weary from the late night. "Mike," he said to the lead man, "why not let these three get some rest? You can take a walk with us, right?"

"Sure, sure, Mr. Erikson."

"Night, boys," Viktor said to the lumbering men.

The two men were led by the bubbling and youthful energy of Morgana. She seemed more like a horse pulling a cart as she dragged them along to Times Square.

"You are acting your age, Viktor. Come along," she teased.

"I am coming," he replied.

Mike snickered to himself at the two in play. It was a side of them not often seen.

When she finally turned the corner, Morgana's eyes were wide, open, and filled with the lights of the square. "Thank you, Mr. Edison." Dashing between cars, Morgana arrived in the center triangle of the square and began to turn in circles, trying to get everything in. Mike and Viktor were able to follow and watch her twirling in the square. "It's so beautiful, Viktor," she said. "Life is so beautiful."

"Mr. Erikson," Mike called out.

Viktor was slow to turn and see that Mike had been hit in a scuffle. It was difficult to understand what was happening. The man standing over Mike with a dark club or bat now looked up to meet Viktor in the eyes. "Mr. Bichel?" Viktor asked. Alaric Bichel stepped over Mike and started to move in as Viktor turned to find Morgana and call out to warn her. "Morgana!"

She stopped twirling to see Viktor calling her. She could see Mike lying on the ground and Alaric Bichel stepping up to Viktor and grabbing him from behind. Morgana felt a sudden burning in her side, and her hand moved down instinctively to touch it. Looking at her hand, she saw that it was covered in brownish liquid.

A soft, husky, and familiar voice whispered closely in Morgana's ear, "This is from Thatch."

Morgana turned to see Elsie Smith, the glint of the lights from Times Square coming off the small blade in her hand. "What have you done?" Morgana asked. "What have you done to me?"

Bichel pulled Viktor's head close and said in hard words, "Watch. Watch your woman die." He held tight as Viktor struggled to break free from his grip.

Morgana put her hand out for help from Viktor before her legs gave way and she tumbled to the ground in a heap.

Viktor was released when a scream in the crowded square filled the air. In the distance, a police whistle blew. Bichel and Smith blended back into the crowd as Viktor grabbed Morgana and took her in his arms. "Morgana," he said, his hand stroking her black hair. "Morgana."

"Viktor? What happened? What?" she asked.

Mike stumbled to his feet amongst the commotion. "Mr. Erikson?"

"Mike. Get the car. We need to get to the hospital," Viktor called to him, and Mike ran off in the direction they had arrived. "Morgana, please do not leave me. You are my everything. You are my all. Hold on. Do not leave me."

Her voice began to fade. "I am not . . . going . . . anywhere."

Viktor tried to remain calm and focused in the moment. He began to rip at her dress to find the bleeding. The soft wet material was difficult to hold, but something in him was able to grab and tear it. Her pale skin now held a slit of red and brown. He put his hand on it and pressed firmly, making her wince. "The car will be here in a minute. We will get you to the hospital. You are going to be all right," Viktor explained.

A squelch of the metal brake only feet away surprised Viktor. It was Mike and his men. Quickly, they picked Morgana up and took her into the back seat.

"Hospital. Now," Mike commanded.

❧ 26 ❧

Recognition

Year 2053
Olivia age 25
Morgana age 27

RECOGNITION IS A strange thing. Something slight triggered her perception. They had never met. She had never seen a picture, but from the description in the book—raven hair, putty skin, her poise, and the traditional elegance in the way she carried herself—Olivia knew. "Morgana?"

Morgana's head tilted at the stranger. "Do we know one another?" Her question hung unanswered in the air. "I see you have been reading Viktor's book. He never goes anywhere without it. Must be some feeling of security in having a thing with you."

"You are Morgana, aren't you?"

"I am, and you are?" Morgana extended her hand in friendship.

"Olivia. I am a volunteer here at St. John's."

Viktor stirred from his bed. "Morgana? Water?"

Morgana looked to the bed, where the husk of Viktor clung to life. "What is his state?"

"He is, well, let me get the doctor to explain. He—"

Morgana interrupted. "I don't want to talk to the doctor. You have been here. You tell me. You understand the situation. You know what a woman needs to hear in a moment like this. Tell me the truth. Spare me the condescension of a man."

Olivia considered her words. She considered all the things she had been reading over the hours to Viktor. Olivia was torn between the reality of Morgana being here and her need for information to make clear decisions for his well-being or peaceful passing. Still, however unlikely, Morgana may be nearly two hundred years old. She may have lived several exciting years and been daughter to a brilliant scientist, a lover of great men, and a suffragette who changed the lives of women for generations.

"He is clinging to his life," she said. "He has been all night. There was little the doctors could do when he was brought in."

"Poor Viktor. Do we know what happened to him?"

"He was part of a hit-and-run incident."

"Did they find the driver?"

"I don't know."

"Could have been anyone," Morgana said dismissively. "So many crazies out there believing what they want about him."

"He keeps asking for you, Morgana, and he keeps asking for water. We have a saline solution running, but he keeps losing water somehow."

"And you have been reading to him?"

"I have." Olivia looked at the book still in her hand. She could feel the buttery texture of the leather, the fine pages at her fingertips.

"He never travels without that book. He loves that book."

"Viktor has been repeating that he can't remember anything. It didn't make sense because he knew the story, but he said he couldn't remember anything. I thought he might have had a blow to the head from the incident." Olivia repeated, "Viktor can't remember anything, he claims, but seems to connect with the story."

"No, Viktor can't really remember anything."

"He can't?" Olivia asked, still looking at the book.

"No."

The click of the deadbolt lock startled Olivia as Morgana secured the door behind her. "Why are you locking the door?"

Morgana went to the window and opened it as far as it would go. It stopped just wide enough to put a hand through. "They fix these so nobody will try to jump out."

"I have watched people try. Some want to run, escape—they think they are trapped." Olivia began to worry at Morgana's strange behavior. Why lock the door? Could she get that door opened again? Could Morgana stop her? Would she?

"Do you mind?" Morgana held up a packet of cigarettes. "I've never been able to kick this habit."

"No, I don't mind. It's a banned substance, but do what you must." Olivia was mesmerized by Morgana's sophistication. She had not seen an actual cigarette since she was a child visiting her great-grandmother.

The way Morgana tapped the box of white sticks, removed one, and lit the tip seemed like something from an early movie. Morgana dragged the smoke into her lungs deeply, held it in for a moment, and exhaled out the slit of open window.

"Why can't Viktor remember anything?" Olivia asked.

"What do you think he would remember? He is an old man."

"And how old are you, Morgana? Are you his daughter?"

Morgana's pursed lips blossomed the full red color of her gloss as she went from blowing smoke to a smile. "I am in my late twenties. Like you?"

"Yes, I am twenty-six."

"Did you go to school to become a nurse?" Morgana guessed.

"I did."

"Then you know there is no scientific evidence that could support what you have been reading to Viktor."

Slightly disappointed with this reply, Olivia needed to ask, "So is it all fiction?"

"Well . . ." Morgana took another hit. "Who knows what the truth is anymore?" She amused herself with the comment. The side of her mouth curled, and she gave a cheesier grin. "You are a very pretty woman, Olivia, if you don't mind me noticing."

"Thank you. I don't mind at all. I must admit I don't feel very pretty tonight. I've been in these scrubs, reading. I could use a hot bath."

"A hot bath sounds nice."

Olivia still wanted more. The parts to this puzzle didn't all fit. "Where did they find you? How did the police contact you to come here?"

"Phone."

"You live nearby? It wasn't difficult to find the hospital?"

"Not far."

"Well, I will let the doctor know you are here, let you have some privacy with Viktor."

"Don't go. Stay. We are having such a nice conversation."

"I should really let him know."

"Please wait until I finish this, at least, before you open the door. The smell will spill out to the hallway, and who needs the grief?"

"Oh, okay. Sure." Olivia sat back in her chair and watched Morgana's delicate fingers manage the cigarette, her lips kissing the filter and drawing in.

Nothing for Morgana seemed a rush. Even as Viktor lay in a hospital bed, his last moments slipping into nothingness, she had all the time in the world. "How far did you get in the book?"

Olivia held the book up again, not thinking of her action. "Viktor and Morgana had just made amends and become friends. It's 1923."

"The roaring twenties." Morgana looked out the window and exhaled. "I like that part: the boom before the bust."

"Do things go awry between the two? Are they not friends? Don't spoil it, please. I've actually gotten really into this book. Sitting here with Viktor, it almost seems real, but . . ."

"The Great Depression, that's the bust. The two remain friends in the story. It's a rather happy ending."

"And in real life?" Olivia asked.

"Well, that's a different story. Are you sure you want to know?"

"I would."

Morgana flicked the cigarette butt out the window and pulled the extra chair up to Olivia's.

Olivia could smell the penetrating odor of smoke on Morgana as she drew closer. It was a combination of old smoke and new smoke mixed with expensive perfume.

Morgana leaned toward Olivia and spoke in steady and certain words, "Parts of the story are absolutely true."

"Like what parts? Did you live together on an estate?"

"Here." Morgana pulled a nearly identical copy of the book from her purse.

Olivia opened the book to the inside cover where there was an inscription that read "Morgana Erikson" written in ink. "Your copy?"

"Indeed. Turn to chapter five."

"There is no chapter five—or six," Olivia explained.

"Not in his copy."

"Is it that horrific?"

"It is for Viktor. It was, at least for a long time, something that haunted him. He claimed he was over it for many years, but he would still wake me in the middle of most nights, calling out for the captain, calling out to his men, trying to stop history."

"And for you?"

"I have to admit, I still have a hard time with it."

"Does your copy have all the chapters?"

"As far as I know." Morgana stood and went to the window, opening her cigarette case again and retrieving the lighter. "Go ahead, read on, and read out loud."

◌ 27 ◌

Chapter Five: Yucatán

Year 1839
Viktor age 20
Morgana age 17

"I T SEEMS MY daughter has taken an interest in you, Mr. Erikson," the doctor said.

Erikson looked up from the campfire to meet the man in the eyes. He studied his expression to measure his words. "She is some woman."

"She is beautiful like her mother—God rest her soul, died giving birth—and smart like me. Best any man could ask for in a daughter."

"A fine lady."

"Well," the doctor added, "she is not really a *lady*, you see. I tried for years to send her to the right schools, instill in her the proper etiquette, and be certain that she was introduced to the right people, but it never really caught on with her to be a lady." He took a sip from the canteen. "I blame myself, really. Too many adventures, too many locations I have dragged her to where being a lady, well, they are not looked on like we see them. Some parts of the world do not respect life, let alone gender."

"I have been to those places."

"So you understand," the doctor said, poking a stick into the embers of the fire. "She can be so strong-willed. She gets that from me too, I suppose. Like this fountain—I have not let go of finding this water her entire life, no matter what others say."

"But you believe that the water is real and something for us to find?"

"With all of my heart and mind. It has to be real, has to be. I just need to find it," de la Motte said.

A rustle in the distance caught the attention of both men, and Erikson was quick to go for his sidearm.

"Stand down, sailor," Durand's voice bellowed in the darkness. "It's only the three of us."

The silhouettes became true images of the captain, Han, and Morgana as they rested comfortably by the fire light.

"The trail disappears not far from here," Durand said.

"What does that mean? Did we take a wrong turn? Miss it?" Erikson asked.

"No, the trail is old. We are close. We will find the second pyramid in the morning light," Han said.

"Close? How close?" the doctor asked.

"Very close. We will need more light," Han said.

"If it's another night on the ground, I am going to get comfortable." Durand unhooked the brown leather straps from his bed roll and smoothed out the the folds before lying down.

Han and the doctor followed the captain's lead while Morgana sat comfortably beside Erikson in the light of the diming fire.

"It has been a long day," she said.

"It will give us more time tomorrow because we pushed hard."

"I don't think I have done this much walking since Father and I were in Egypt. Even then, there was always the option to get on one of those filthy camels."

At the first sounds of snoring from Durand, Erikson took the small gentle hand of Morgana into his own. He could feel the jump in his heart at the touch her flesh. Erikson had fought and killed men, survived being chased by the crown, and stared down death in a tempest, yet it took more courage than he had ever summoned to look her in the eyes.

At first, she was surprised to feel his rough hand holding hers. She thought it might be a jungle creature about to strike. Seeing it was him, the effort of affection being made, his deep blue eyes penetrating into her very soul, she began to melt.

The two connected in that moment, in something bigger than individuals. Beyond the time they lived or the distances traveled, it had brought them here to this moment, together. They leaned into one another, closing the gap, and kissed.

"I suppose there is something about a beautiful woman that makes a man feel he has to protect her," Durand said, and Viktor smiled without saying a word. It was more than the smile Durand had seen hundreds of times. "Well, if that doesn't say it all," Durand added.

With a tug at the back end of his glove, the blade fitting perfectly in his hand, Viktor began to hack at the thick foliage of the jungle where the path ended. For every five swings, he would step back and Durand would pick up where Viktor had stopped. The rhythm created by the two men became hypnotic in the early morning light. The "swack, swack, swack, swack, swack" followed by the "hack, hack, hack, hack, hack" eventually woke the three still in slumber by the cold ashes of last night's fire. Han was quick to leap to his feet, pack his sleeping roll, and find his saber to join the men, while the doctor and Morgana were slower to get up and going.

By the time the two de la Mottes had reached the three men of the *Ponthieva*, several extra yards had been added to the trail. It had disturbed the lives of many insects and small jungle creatures into a frenzy. While unpleasant, it did not detour them from blazing this trail forward.

It was Han who took the swing with a definitive ping against the sheer face of stone, breaking the "swack" and "hack" rhythm.

"Sounded like a shovel hitting buried treasure," Viktor said.

With a series of more hacks into the green and brown plant life, the three were able to clear away the centuries of growth.

"If it were easier to find, someone would have already found it," Durand said.

"*If* this is it," Viktor quipped. "We might just be doing some much-needed gardening."

"Look at the beauty of this." The doctor's hand inspected the surface. "This is no accident or pile of rubble. These rocks were cut, placed with care, not with mortar but carefully sculpted and set into place by design."

They all looked at the details unnoticed until pointed out, how the moss-laden stone was shaped into unnatural sharp angles, creating a slanted rise in pattern.

"Let's find the corners," Durand said.

Han and Durand went right while Viktor went left. The doctor followed the two men, picking up cuttings and throwing them aside, and Morgana followed Viktor to do the same.

When the heat of the jungle began to catch up with the laboring men, Durand called out "break" to stop everyone and regroup at the entry point they had cleared hours earlier.

From his sack, Han removed cloth-wrapped food comprised of spiced meats and old bread. With a clean blade, he cut a serving for each, starting with Morgana.

"We could be here a long time just making our way through the growth," Durand said.

"Would have been easier with ten men," Viktor replied.

"Not worth the time to go get them."

"Han, how much rope do we have?" Viktor asked.

Han looked to the bag strapped around his torso and removed a sizable coil of good, thick rope he'd brought from the *Ponthieva*.

Viktor showed teeth with a bitter grin. "That looks to be enough."

After the meal and a good rest, Han uncoiled the rope, re-coiled it with a loose knot holding it in place, and then set it around the neck and torso of Viktor. It was loose enough to allow him to move but close enough that it wouldn't get in the way of his ascent.

"And just where do you think you are going?" Morgana asked.

He pointed. "Up there."

"It must be twenty feet if not more. You'll break your neck."

"If you stand right there, you can break my fall," he replied. His smile portrayed confidence in the plan. "I am a sailor, Morgana. I spend most of my days climbing up and down the mast. I was raised on a ship and have been climbing like a monkey all my life."

"It is true, ma'am. Mr. Erikson is the second best climber the *Ponthieva* has," Durand said.

"Second?" Viktor asked.

Durand gave that rare gift of a smile to Viktor, who turned to find a grip.

The stone cutters of the region were highly skilled centuries ago. Viktor cursed them as he fought for every inch up the wall, looking for the smallest seam to press his fingertips against. From a morning filled with cutting and the strain of climbing, his arms began that uncontrollable shake of muscles near exhaustion. The very lip of his boot found an eyelash width of an edge, allowing him to rest a moment, still too far from the top.

Stuck in the moment, he knew the words Morgana spoke were true: at this height, falling would kill him, or worse, leave him crippled, forcing the captain to put a shot in his head rather than leave him for dead. The only way to live was to move up.

In all the stretching, pulling, and finding space for footing, he slowly made way. With one final reach, he thought he had discovered the top only to find a loose rock. Its wobble caused a sting of panic to shoot through his body. As it loosened from the edge, his release dropped it in place, forcing a desperate grab at the ledge. With the thrush of his legs on a slick green face, Viktor scurried up over the edge in a final burst of energy he did not believe he had left in him.

"What happened? I can't see him," Morgana said.

"Give him a moment. I am sure he is catching his breath, my dear," the doctor said.

"It was not easy what he just did. Any other man might be dead at our feet right now," Durand added.

At their relief, the tip of the rope landed at their feet as the length smacked against the stone surface. Silently, the other end of the rope slowly lowered to within reach.

"You are first, ma'am," Durand said.

Han finished the knot around Morgana before joining the other three. They began to pull at their end. Hand over hand, the rope moved through the arms of the men pulling.

Morgana moved up the face of the stone with a gentle, effortless motion. She turned to face the edge at the top and pulled herself over to find that Viktor had been using a giant stone in the shape of an ancient god as an anchor to help pull her up. "Well, that's a neat trick," she said.

"Good to see you made it," he replied. Extracting the rope tied around her, he dropped the end and repeated the effort until they were all reunited atop the structure.

The vantage point from the top confirmed climbing had been the best option. It was not a pyramid but an arena. The only visible steps led down to the center. Intricately crafted stone faces looked inward, observing the action on the field, with two stone platforms, each with a perfectly rectangular monolith stone sitting on top.

"Sacrificial alters?" Durand asked.

"My first thought seeing them too," Viktor replied. "You would think a table shape would be better for that, the way they stand upright."

"Chain them up standing then?" Durand said.

"We will see," Viktor said, moving forward. "At least we get steps for this part."

The five made way down to the arena floor cautiously, carefully watching for loose stones and the unexpected.

De la Motte removed a book from his satchel and began to take notes. Another book he carried for reference included the writings and translations he had been making for decades. Invested hours spent in libraries, journeys half way around the globe, and expeditions taking him away from a society that thought him wasteful on the effort were finally paying off.

"Syzygy," the doctor proclaimed.

"What was that word?" Durand asked.

"Syzygy, the alignment of three bodies." The doctor thought for better words. "It is a conjunction of opposing forces. It is the yoking or paring together of the bodies."

"Congruence," Han added, "when the earth, the moon, and the sun align—this is how we know this word in navigation."

"Yes, Mr. Han, correct. But here we are bringing together powerful bodies. Here is life and death, side by side, in balance next to one another."

"Life and death?" Durand asked.

"Yes, these are not places for sacrifice; they are the fountains of life and death." De la Motte went up to the steps of the closest stone platform and pointed to the small spot where a rust-colored pattern started to spread on the stone monolith. "The source of the water, the water of life."

"Dear Lord, he did it. He found the fountain of youth," Durand said to Morgana.

"Oh, Daddy, you did it!" Her voice rose. "You proved them wrong. You found it after all these years."

"I did it," the doctor said with satisfaction. "I found it."

"Well," Viktor said, "you found the fountain. Where is the gold? That's why I came along."

"Gold? You ask for gold at the moment of our greatest discovery? I have given you too much credit, Mr. Erikson. You are a small-minded man to think only of treasure in terms of gold," de la Motte scolded.

With an even tone to counter the doctor's passion, Viktor replied, "You have found a pair of water fountains. There is nothing to prove your ideas about life and death."

"Mr. Erikson," Durand barked, "why don't you take a rest? You must be exhausted. Look around for gold, if you like, and find a way out of here besides that rope."

"Aye" was all Viktor said. He walked back up the steps to the top rim and sat in the shade of the head of an ancient deity. He took some of the smoked meat from his satchel and drank some water. This was followed by a pinch of salt to help balance his spirits as he rested. From this height, Viktor watched the doctor find a stick in the growth and poke at the fountain's hole until a steady stream of water began to flow. He then went to the other monolith and repeated the action.

Pools of water had gathered on the platforms during Viktor's sleep. They began to resemble one of the Zen fountains of Asia or of the classic design in Italy. From this vantage, he could see the shadow cast from the stone as a sun dial. It had grown late in the day, and unless they pushed forward, they would spend the night here.

"Feeling better?" Morgana asked, and Viktor looked up to see that sometime during his slumber, she had joined him in the shade. "Seems like you picked the best spot here," she added.

"What is your father up to?"

"He is reading the text around the fountains."

"More text?"

"He is not certain which is the fountain of life and which is death."

"Kind of an important point to know."

"The text," she explained, "is not specific enough, or his notes on the matter are not precise. Death and life seem to be rather close in symbols."

"Not a mistake you would want to make."

"No, not one I want him to make. I suppose there is a chance," she mused.

"What chance is that?"

"Well, say he gets it wrong. I lose my father, but we know the other fountain is the right one. If he gets it right, I keep my father, but what do you do with the water from the other fountain?"

"What do you do with it? I don't understand."

"Father's going to take samples, study the waters, and test the waters in a scientific process, in a series of controlled environments. What did you think he was going to do with the waters?"

He gave her that devilish grin again and said. "I am here for the gold. I have all the water I need."

"I would live forever," she replied.

"You would?"

"If I had the water of life and it let you stay young, I would be. You don't know what it is like to be a woman in this time, in this world. I need to be escorted to dinner or to the store. Someone needs to be at my side always. My mind is keen and sharp, but few care for what I say or think. My body is for child rearing, and the best I can hope for is a man of means to care for me. But I wasn't designed to be like that. Ask me to sew a button, bake a cake, or entertain you in a song and I am lost. If you want to discuss the tribes of Africa, the history of Europe, or the importance of an observation method in science, you have come to the right person."

"Your father wants to test the waters, and you want to drink the water and live forever."

"Yes, and you want gold, a good drink, and a good time."

"Well, as long as we are clear," he said.

"We are clear."

Getting to his feet took the aid of the statue's face as the soreness in his back had gathered in slumber. Once there, he stretched a bit before offering his hand to Morgana. The two walked the upper edge of the arena, looking out to the jungle between the tree tops and searching for an exit point or path they had not already lain. There were areas of high density growth like the one they had traversed and areas that looked less dense in small patches.

One of the less dense patches seemed to be near one of the recesses on the same level as the platform. The two made their way down the stairs on the end closest to the patch and found the recess in the arena's design. It was an entry point to the arena floor that was a walled front which, unless you were standing at it to see the clear and open corridor to the outside, looked like part of the interior.

"So clever, these stone cutters," she said, stepping out of sight from the others.

Natural light extended only a few feet into the corridor from either end. They stood at the one end and could see light at the other, but there was too much darkness between. From his satchel, he removed his packet of matches and struck the friction point, igniting the wooden stick. A flare of light and they could see the torches along the wall. With a second stick from the box, he ignited the nearest torch on the wall, taking it in hand.

Slowly, the two made way down the corridor, igniting torch after torch on the wall and driving back the darkness until they were on the other side, back in the heat of the jungle, where an old path pointed away.

"Well, at least we won't have to go down that rope," said Viktor.

"Let's try that other corridor," she said.

"Other corridor?"

"Well, there was another recessed wall. I assume it leads somewhere."

Upon exploration, she was correct. The other recess in the arena wall was another corridor, but this one went to a room, not an exit. Once the room was lit, the two discovered it was a place for preparation. Golden headdresses, jeweled religious artifacts, and masks from the place of worship from centuries past were now placed in a sack for easy transport. A pig-size golden statue, too heavy for the sack, was tied with a rope and dragged to the arena center, where the others had begun to make camp for the night.

"You find what you were looking for?" Durand asked.

"And more," said Viktor. "Enough to make the trip worth our while and more."

"Sit. Join us. We were just discussing the fountains," Durand said.

With a sense of finality, Viktor dropped to the dirt from a day filled with chopping, climbing, dragging, and carrying the weight of the expedition.

"Dr. de la Motte was just talking us through his transcriptions," Han said.

"Yes, the words describing the two fountains are similar in some ways but very different in others, so it will be difficult to tell which is the fountain of life and which is death without testing it."

"Testing it in a laboratory back at the university is what my father means," Morgana added.

"Well, actually," Durand said, "your father was saying that a field test was going to tell us more."

"Madness," Viktor said. "Why would you put your life at risk for this? You have no idea what the results of drinking either of those two waters will be. At best, it is just ordinary, plain water. At worst, you die because you couldn't decipher what some crazy people chipped into stone. And if you don't die right away, you might get septic—we'd have to carry you back to the ship to die." Viktor brought silence to the fire ring.

"But if it is the water of life, the fountain of youth . . ." de la Motte whispered.

"I will give you that, Doctor. You have been right up to this point," Viktor said. "But is it worth the risk of your daughter losing her father? Lord knows I am not the first one who is drinking that water."

$\backsim$ 28 $\backsim$

Chapter Six: El Redondel

Year 1839
Viktor age 20
Morgana age 17

S HOTS FIRED IN the distance awoke them in the dark night. Viktor and Durand were first to the top of the arena. Spyglasses in hand, both scooting to the edge on their bellies, they could make out a campfire with a large force of men around it. The sounds of drunken merriment and celebratory gunplay rose above the tree line to where the two men perched in wait.

"Federales?" Durand asked. "Republicans?"

Another plume of smoke in the distance followed the crack of a shot fired.

"Who cares?" Viktor said. "Looks like they are here for the night."

Both moved slowly from the edge and returned to the others, who were already packing the camp to run away into the darkness if needed.

"What is it?" Morgana asked.

"Could be *federales*, maybe republicans. They have set camp for the night not far from here," Viktor said.

She followed with "Are we safe?"

"Only if they don't find this place," Durand said.

"One path in, one rope out," Viktor said.

"No good choice," Durand said. "Let's be ready to move quickly."

"I can take first watch," said Han.

Durand nodded affirmation and returned to his bedding. "Better rest while we can"

———————

It could have been the jab to his belly from the end of the rifle barrel or the kick to his head from the boot, but the doctor woke with a surprised yelp that stirred the others. In the moon's light, they could see from the uniform the man was wearing that he was Mexican regular army.

"*Muévete*," he said, followed by a grunt. "*Muévete*." In return, he received a puzzled expression from de la Motte. "*Levántate*," he said, but the doctor lay motionless in place.

Durand lit a match and set it to the fire ring, bringing light to the situation.

Viktor said with the calmness of a professional, "He wants you to stand up, Doctor."

Slowly, that fatherly man got his feet under him. In the movement it took to steady himself from the knee, rising from the waist, de la Motte grabbed at the musket. With a flare, the firearm thundered. The close proximity of the shot tore through de la Motte, his skin and clothes catching fire. His scream of pain was second to Morgana's scream of the horror of watching her father murdered.

Viktor was first to his feet, first to the solider, and quick to remove the gun. Han, from out of the darkness, struck a blow so hard to the back of the man's head it knocked the red ribbon off his blue cap and sent him 'ed to the ground.

"an, where were you?" Durand demanded.

"Fell asleep," Han said.

"Go check the entrance. Make certain no one followed," Durand said.

Morgana rested her father's head in her lap as he gasped for air. His hand clutched at the opening in his chest, where parts of his lung and guts fluttered with the last of his shallow breaths. His mouth moved, he wanted to speak, but there wasn't enough air coming out the right end for the vocal cords to make a sound. His lips moved to form his last four words: "Morgana, I love you."

She watched the last life leave as his eyes went to a blank stare off into the distance. She looked up to Viktor. There were no tears, only anger. She laid his head gently to the ground and saw the glint of the fire reflecting off the Colt Patterson in Viktor's holster. She jumped to her feet in a rush of passion and stripped the sidearm from his waist. Morgana marched to the injured soldier and stood over him. She kicked him until he stirred.

Durand and Erikson were close by in observation, not interference.

The soldier opened his eyes, and a flash of fear came across his face as he realized what had happened, the dilemma he was in.

"Up," she instructed, but his expression did not change. *"Muévete!"* she screamed, which brought him to his feet immediately. With the barrel of the Colt Patterson pointed at his back, she jabbed and prodded him in the direction of the fountain on the far end.

"What are you doing?" Durand asked.

"We have our test subject. He became a subject when he entered the arena. He volunteered when he shot my father. And now," she jabbed him harder, pushing him in place, "he will drink. *Toma!*"

The solider understood. With large sorrowful eyes, he turned to look at her. Pointing to the water, he asked, *"Toma?"*

She gritted her teeth and said, *"Toma."*

He looked frightened at the stone fountain. With another highly persuasive jab at the back, the man stumbled forward, nearly standing in the pool that had gathered from the open trickle. He cupped his hands beneath the spout and collected a mouthful. A slurp sounded and the water consumed. He stood, looked at the three, and waited.

"Well?" Durand asked. "Now what?"

"I don't know. Father did not know. That is why he is testing it."

The man stood before them, unchanged and carrying an expression of uncertainty and fear. Then, there was a twinge of pain and a tick of the eye, and whatever was going to happen seemed to begin. A groan escaped from the man as he clenched at his belly. He coiled into a tight ball and started to scream. As he writhed in pain, the two men watched in disgust while Morgana smiled at the delight of his suffering.

The soldier's moans began to intensify. An animal cry screeched from the man as he tossed to his side. Undone from his fetal coil, he reached out to the men, inching closer, driving them back in fear of his touch. Boils began to form on his skin; discolored patches formed on his face.

In a moment of instinctive mercy, Viktor took the outstretched hand. The hand in his melted away like the meat of an over-ripened peach basking in the hot sun.

Even Morgana, who had enjoyed the revenge of the suffering man, cringed to see him begin to melt before her eyes.

The mushy hand gone, his arm followed. Soiled stains on the pants were all that remained of his legs when his screams had gurgled away into the final "pop" of the man's form. The syrupy uniform was all that was left.

Durand turned to Viktor and said, "I think that was the fountain of death."

"He got what he deserved," Morgana said.

"That is just mean, Morgana. No one deserved that death," Durand replied.

"For killing my father, that man did."

"You are acting as if you enjoyed that display," he said.

She turned to Viktor. "It looks as if I may be good at something."

Viktor did not know what to say to this woman and her newfound ⌐or killing.

"What was all that yelling?" Han said on return. "That camp of soldiers must have heard." He looked to the blob of fizzing protoplasm the soldier's uniform lay in. "What is that? Where did our prisoner go?"

"That is him. He drank the water from that fountain." Viktor pointed.

"So this must be the fountain of life," Han said to Durand.

The two looked at each other, processing the question in their own minds. What would the fountain of life bring? Would it be the opposite of the fountain of death? Would it mean immortality? Was it worth the risk?

The two dashed to the opposite fountain. Like children, they pushed and wrestled to be the next one to drink, to gain the water of life. Han drank first. He had filled his cupped hands, and began to drink. Durand watched, then lapped at his own hands for the water of life. Triumphant, the two men looked to one another having finished the deed.

"No, no, what have you done?" Viktor called out to his crewmates. "What did you do?"

The smiles on the faces of Han and Durand were satisfying.

"It tastes sweet," Han said.

Durand said, "Must be the fountain of life."

They were fueled with the sense of excitement and desire from all the stories the doctor had told during the journey and the nights falling to sleep in their bunks, dreaming of what the water might accomplish, but the wonders of the unknown possibilities now passed. The realization came across the two faces of the men at nearly the same time. They looked to the fountain, questioning what they had done. What power had come over them that had made them leap before looking?

The smiles soon vanished from the faces of both men. Cries of pain carried out across the arena floor as the two writhed in pain on the stone alters under the watchful eyes of the ancient stone-faced gods, unmoved by another sacrifice made before them.

Viktor turned away, covering Morgana's view and looking her in the eyes. "Think of something else, think of the happiest time in your life, imagine you are somewhere else, and focus on my voice. We are going to survive this night."

As he tried to gain her attention, block the reality of the moment, she asked coldly, "To what end?"

Her question brought a clarity to the moment. He set her aside and took back his sidearm from her hand. The Colt Patterson felt heavy in his hand as he approached the two men clenched in the struggling torture from the water. Drawing the hammer back to click and cock and then taking a close bead on Durand's head, Viktor observed the miraculous transformation as the old man he had known minutes ago was now young and getting younger in appearance. His aim turned to silence Han only to find the same wonders taking place on his body: a transformation from man to child to infant.

"Do it!" Morgana yelled. "Put them out of their misery." She could not see what was happening, only hear the sounds of pain cry out. "They will hear them, find us, take your gold, and kill us," Morgana said. With each step away from the fountain of death, away from the juicy remains of her father's killer, and toward the fountain of life, she could see why Viktor hesitated. This was different than what had happened to her father.

"Stay back," Viktor said. He raised his hand to signal for her to stop.

Morgana ignored his instruction to get a better view. Seeing the last moments of the transformation, she turned, darted back to the campfire, and began to dig out her father's canteen, emptying it onto the fire. Next, she found Han's and did the same, finally repeating this with Durand's tin. Her pace quickened to the fountain of death.

Viktor watched. "What are you doing?"

"I am going to gather water from the fountains," she said.

"Why in God's name would you want to capture death? What could you ever do with water from that fountain?" Viktor asked. The screams and crying ended, Viktor holstered his gun. He took the infants and began to swaddle each in the shirts they wore as men. Then, he gathered the belongings of each man and bagged them as well. He could hear her steps as she dashed to the fountain of life and filled two of the canteens.

Morgana was cautious with the waters. Her hands wrapped in handkerchiefs, she removed every drop on the pressed tin before carefully retuning each to the fabric-strapped wrapping that captured condensation and moisture. Just for safe keeping, she marked the canteen from the water of death with an *X* from the ashes of the campfire.

Taking the pants each man had worn, Viktor turned them into swaddled slings, the bulk of the fabric holding the infant in place with the legs tied tightly over the shoulder to hold them in place. Both he and Morgana would carry one each. Then, Viktor picked up the sack of treasure and began to make difficult choices. The statue would have been a prize that two adult men could drag but would now be left behind. Jewels he could carry, but the bulky gold parts would need to stay behind with the statue.

A path for departure was the next decision that had to be made. "From the sounds of the shots, leaving via the corridor would take us right to the camp," he said.

"So it's back down the rope?" she asked.

"Which means you will have to be able to hold yourself. I can't lower you and the babies down by myself," he said.

"I don't know if I can."

"You will have to, or at least fall gracefully."

"I don't know if I can," she repeated.

"What happened to that girl who boarded the *Ponthieva* that we were going to have a hard time keeping up with?"

"Harrumph" was the noise she made. Her Southernness flared and her head tilted up in indignation that she could not do something a man could do.

Viktor and Morgana made their way up the steps again with baby Han and baby Durand strapped close to their chests. Viktor dropped the rope over the side with the bag of treasure tied to the end as a weight to keep steady.

"Just focus on the moment," he said. "Hold the rope, slide down the rope hand over hand, let out a little slack, keep the balls of your feet against the wall, and walk backwards. You can do this," Viktor encouraged.

Getting over the edge, taking position, and overcoming that mental hurdle to perform such an unintuitive action were the most difficult parts for Morgana. When Viktor yelled "go" the third time, she began her descent. Her hands burned immediately going down, her feet strained against the wall to stay parallel, and in fear of dropping too far down, she ended up landing on her bottom now wet and soiled from the jungle floor.

Viktor was quick down the rope when he heard that she had landed. In moments of his feet landing, he had the bag of treasure tied and on his back. "It's going to be another long day," he said. Viktor helped her to her feet and tightened the loads they now carried. "You are going to have to show me that same spirited gumption to get home."

Morgana nodded.

"If you get tired, tell me. If you need to stop, speak up. But if I tell you to be quiet, you will need to be."

Morgana nodded again in understanding before he took her arm and hurried her down the path they had cut the morning before. The sun began to rise and the first rays of light from a new day peaked through the trees as Viktor set a brisk pace down the old path they had taken the day prior. There were times when the two stopped cold to listen before moving on. When they heard voices in the distance or the snap of a branch, they were quick to squat low below brush or behind a tree.

It seemed to last forever in Morgana's mind. Each step slogged on at a relentless pace that pushed her body in new ways it had never known. During a quick rest, she realized just how easy Durand and his crew had made her life during the expedition. Someone had carried her pack, and another carried her water. Now they were moving at a much slower rate.

"I know it's difficult, but you are doing wonderfully," Viktor said.

She found comfort in his words. She knew he was an excellent shot, stronger than most, and smart enough to circumnavigate any troubles. If there were any one person on this expedition she could trust with her life it was Viktor Erikson.

At long last, they made their way back to the pyramid where only a week earlier she had found comfort in the night resting on his shoulder. So much had transpired over those days. Her world had changed.

"We are going to rest here for a few hours," he said.

"Finally."

"I think we lost the army troops from the arena, so we can afford a short rest. You lie here with the babies and treasure for a bit. I am going to make certain that the crew left a skiff for us."

She was too tired to say anything. Instead, she watched as Viktor went across the opening in the jungle in the direction of the river. The babies cooed a little but seemed occupied. Her eyes grew heavy, and in moments, her struggle to keep them open was gone. Sleep had won the battle.

Morgana did not recognize her surroundings when she woke in the darkness from Viktor shaking her. She sat up and realized that she was on the bottom stone step where she had fallen asleep with the babies in the sunlight of the day. "What?"

Viktor hushed her. "I think there are people here, natives." He picked up the babies gently and wrapped them again in the swaddle and ties—one with Morgana and the other to himself. Slowly, silently, they made their way along the edge of the pyramid, through the cut trail they had blazed as a team, and to the skiff the crew had left for them. With everyone inside and settled, Viktor pushed them off the shore and allowed the currents to carry them.

Suddenly, a male voice called out from the shore in an unknown language. It stirred other voices into a chorus of replies.

"They saw us," Viktor said. He pulled one of the ores out from the bottom of the skiff and started to push the little boat ahead of the pace of the current.

"Can we out run them?"

"We will see," he said.

∞ 29 ∞

Shadow Witch

Year 2053
Olivia age 25
Morgana age 27

"IT SOUNDS HORRIFIC—YOUR father's death, the soldier's screams. It's no wonder Viktor wanted those pages removed," Olivia said.

Starting her fifth cigarette at the window, Morgana said, "I wouldn't want to live that day again. And I didn't want this Viktor to carry the pain."

"This Viktor?" Olivia asked.

Morgana looked at the book in Olivia's hand and its nearly identical twin on the table. "You see, there are many truths in the book. I met Viktor in Savannah, we sailed on a ship south, and my father died finding the waters of life and death as described in all the gory details." Morgana took another drag.

"Where does the story become fiction? What is missing?"

"You asked me why Viktor cannot remember."

Olivia nodded. "Yes."

"The man in this bed is not Viktor. Well, not the original Viktor." The devilish grin returned, both frightening and hypnotic with power. "A goddess needs to conserve her resources. You see, there is only so much water, so much treasure, and I am not one to share her throne with just anyone."

From Olivia's expression, it seemed to take a moment for the words to translate into meaning for her.

Morgana added, "This man you have been spending the evening with must be the fourth or fifth Viktor—I cannot recall. So many accidents happen over the years."

"This is not Viktor?"

"He is *a* Viktor, not *the* Viktor."

"I don't understand. What happened to *the* Viktor?" Olivia asked.

"What did that mustached bastard Friedrich Nietzsche say? 'What is done out of love always takes place beyond good and evil.' Viktor, the original Viktor, did not share the same evils, so I have been instilling them in the Viktors that followed."

Olivia found it difficult to believe what she was hearing. "You have been instilling evil in the new Viktors? Why?"

"I just couldn't forgive him for what happened to Alice. I tried. For so many years I tried. I tried very hard to find forgiveness in my heart. No matter how I looked, it wasn't there. Alice was so much more to me. She was my everything."

"How did you do it?" Olivia asked.

"We were going through so much of the water of life, and the flask with the *X* was still full. When it came time, Viktor was given water from the wrong flask." She feigned an expression of confusion. "Oops, silly girl." She smiled. "There was no body, no evidence, just a stain that was eventually scrubbed clean. It may be difficult to believe, but there was a time when orphanages were filled with little boy babies that had blond hair and blue eyes. It was easy to raise one as Viktor."

"And when they couldn't remember?"

"Well, that's when the book became so handy. Writers, hungry writers, can shape a tale into something better. We, the original Viktor and I, met Autor Widmor on our trip to Europe in the 1930s. We spent a good amount of time each night drinking, telling tales, and sharing our story. Viktor was rather loose-tongued when he started to drink. Autor was very hungry in those days, needed money to run away from Poland or something. He was happy to write down every word we paid for." Morgana flicked the butt out the window into the night. She took the chair next to Olivia and propped her feet up on Viktor's bed, across Olivia's lap, trapping her in place.

"The book is enough for a little boy to believe," Morgana continued explaining. "I could read to them each night about what brave man they had been. The first quarter of the book is all about ships, strong men, adventures, and fun. The Viktors loved how they had lived. Still, there are only so many adventures, so many times you can drink from the water without losing something, a detail here, a decade there. As they get older, little boys understand that memories fade, can get lost in time, dementia, memory loss—wiggle room to get them to do what you need. Viktor, *the* Viktor, was still very sharp in the days we were with Autor Widmor. Unlocked him with a few drinks, and everything poured out. I have always been grateful that our story was captured down in writing."

Olivia tried to understand what Morgana described as being real, that there was a fountain, a water of life, an elixir of death, and this woman, who embodied the *Ponthieva*, a shadow witch with her potions and spells, had toyed with so many lives and killed so many.

"All the stories in this book are true?"

"Mostly. I needed the baby Viktors to regard me, to love me"—her voice switched from her slow and Southern tone to one of anger—"and to give me back all that treasure."

It suddenly clicked in Olivia's head. "You needed the babies for the money. Viktor cut you out; he took you out of the game."

"Viking bastard," Morgana nearly spat. "He took away Alice, the gold, the jewels, the money, the properties, everything. He held it over me, doled it out to me, gave me a scant allowance to try and get by. He was a miser who held on to every penny with a tight fist and surrounded himself with lawyers to keep it hidden away from me. Viktor spent it on puerile passings, like establishing this hospital, trusts, and foundations that funneled the money, my money, to all these perishable people."

"You raised the babies to believe they were *the* Viktor, that they couldn't remember the past lives, but you knew," Olivia said. "You could remember."

"Every detail, every moment, I still carry them all with me. More a burden than a blessing. Arrogant years when I played the goddess without abandon, giving people a second chance in life."

"It sounds like a little regret may be in there."

"Maybe a few. Immortality makes for strange bedfellows."

Olivia took a moment to see the predicament she was now in. "Do you intend to give this Viktor from the water of death?"

Morgana reached into her purse on the floor and produced a tin flask with a black *X* marked on the side. She shook it a little for dramatic effect and flashed her sinister smile. "Just in case." She dropped it on top of her bag. "This Viktor," Morgana said, "was a decent Viktor."

The Viktor in the hospital bed, who had been listening in silence the entire time, began to weep.

"Oh, honey." Morgana stood and leaned over to touch his check under the bandage-wrapped head. "Take comfort in the thought that I didn't have to give you the water from the bad flask. You will just die on your own. It will be completely natural. So much more peaceful for all of us that way. Less to clean up for your nurse friend."

"A decent Viktor? Aside from the treasure, were the others bad to you?" Olivia asked. She remained in the chair, noticing the flask with the water of death was within reach as Morgana stood with her back to her.

Morgana looked over this Viktor with a careful eye. "Some of them were a little too touchy when I was young or forced themselves on me at times when I wasn't willing."

With Morgana still hunched over Viktor, Olivia quietly attempted to remove the flask marked with an *X* from Morgana's bag. With each subtle movement, she thought she was causing the loudest noises that would surely catch that shadow witch's attention. On her third attempt at a slow and silent maneuver, she could feel the cool metal press in the palm of her hand, hidden from view.

Morgana carried on, "Other Viktors treated me like a child or a sub-ordinate, not a partner, not a companion. The worst of them thought they could spend *my* money and I wouldn't notice. Those Viktors got a sweet drop or two during the next meal and died in horrible agony. No carpeting at our house, all marble and wood—much easier to clean."

Olivia saw the syringe on top of the table next to the bed. It was in reach. As Morgana, enthralled in her narcissistic stories, carried on, Olivia simply reached out and took it. Her quick movement made Olivia realize just how loud and noisy the sterilized paper wrapping sounded, but it had happened so fast, it went unnoticed. The wrapping was similar to that of a Band-Aid: two pieces of paper pressed along the sides in a seam. Unlike the adhesive bandages, which were flat, the syringe had a pocket side, the other flat. It was this pocket that crinkled at the slightest movement.

She felt the item in hand as the anxiety and adrenaline raced in her body, perspiration and moisture gathering in her palms. While Morgana droned on over Viktor's bedside, Olivia's fingertip tickled the edge of the seam. While her face looked forward, she imagined what that edge looked like. In her mind's eye, she could see the blue paper she had handled hundreds of times. The little space of the white paper that left a gap. The red string next to it to help tear it apart in one quick and smooth movement. Her index fingernail tip found the opening. She moved it forward, knowing that the wrapper's edge would work open. Quickly, her index finger moved from right to left, contorted in a curled grip, opening the edge of the wrapping and causing a severe paper cut in the tender skin under her fingernail. Inside, she wanted to scream in pain but fought the urge. Inside, she wanted to declare victory for opening the wrapper with hardly a noise.

Her grip-shaped hand tilted down, and she could feel the plunger of the syringe slide and press against the side of her hand. Gravity helped to drop it out of the wrapper and into her hand. The medical device held in the tips of her fingers, she simply let go of the wrappings and allowed them to silently float to the floor.

Morgana, continuing to lean over Viktor's bedside, spoke in the soothing voice a mother might have for a child, "But this Viktor was kind and good, like a Viktor should be. He found all the accounts, secret and veiled, all those little places where one can hoard away gold coins, bars, or bricks. He found every gem, stone, and diamond and signed them all back to me on his death." She turned back to Olivia with a smile. "Now I alone, Morgana, own all the riches, all the land, all the property, all the treasure . . . once Viktor dies. We prefer to keep a body this time, in your hospital, all nice for the records." Morgana returned to her relaxed and comfortable posture in the seat with her legs across Olivia's lap and said, "It took nearly a century, but its mine, all mine."

"Congratulations," Olivia said. "You must be satisfied reaching your goal." She felt the metal grit of the top of the tin container twisting as she returned it to a tightened state in the hand hidden far away from Morgana's sight.

"But it's not just my goal, Olivia. It should be the goal of all women everywhere. Take back what is rightfully ours. You could share in this with me. The world is yours for only a season, my dear. It would be tragic for a pretty girl like you to realize this too late to enjoy it. Join me for a drink—rather yet, join me for a hot bath. I need a new companion, a real partner. It can be awfully lonely to be a goddess if you don't have someone with you. Plus, you already know the truth, so I won't have to try to convince you."

Olivia considered the offer with a smile. "There have been times when I have been so poor. I have had to work hard and long days to get by."

"Yes, yes, I understand, my sweet girl." Morgana patted her shoulder.

Olivia thought about the difficulty of nursing school, but remembered the rewards of that hard work just the same. She thought back to the years spent caring for her siblings, about the family she had run from to gain a better life. There were reasons why she left and became independent. She remembered the bad man she had just left who had tried to control her, who only a short time ago had stood over her with bloody fists, blaming her for making him angry. "You know, there are so many times I have found myself running away, poor, uncertain of my future," Olivia explained.

"And I can make that all better," Morgana said. She rose from the chair, lifted her bag from the floor, and placed the strap across her shoulder. Her hand reached out to Olivia. "Come with me. I need a partner, a friend, perhaps a lover."

"That all sounds so nice," Olivia said. She took Morgana's hand and followed her guidance to the door.

Morgana unlocked the deadbolt and turned back to Olivia to say, "We are going to have so much fun together," but before Morgana could complete the sentence, Olivia struck her in the neck with the skill of a serpent. The syringe, driven deep into her neck, had fully discharged from the plunger's pressed position.

In an instant, Morgana's face went from joy to confusion. "What have you done?" Morgana asked.

Olivia stepped back.

"What have you done?" she repeated louder. Morgana's hand swatted at the stick in her neck to no avail.

Olivia took another step backward.

When Morgana attempted to follow, she found her legs would not abide her command. They became weak and useless. Morgana clutched her gut, buckled under gravity's law, and coiled into an embryotic position on the floor. She wrestled with the pain, refusing to call out, and only took short, unfulfilling breaths as she writhed. Her will began to win, and Morgana straightened out, her hand reaching for Olivia while she crawled on her belly across the floor, pulling herself along, fighting for every inch.

Olivia found herself retreating in small steps until she was at Viktor's side near the corner. He had been watching the moment play out. With all the will he could muster, Viktor reached out from the bed, his arm stretched to its limit, nearly rolling out, and pulled on the closest monitor. It toppled over, falling on Morgana's dissolving body, and with a pop, her skin burst like an overfilled water balloon, spilling its contents.

Olivia grabbed Viktor before he could lose his balance and tumble to the floor. She safely helped him return to his comfortable position in bed. Her breathing was short and rapid and her hands trembling, but the effects of the adrenalin pulsing through her veins began to subside as the reality of the moment set in.

The door swung open, and the face of the floor nurse looked in. "What's going on in here? What was all that noise?"

Olivia, still shaken, recovered by saying, "There's been a small accident. Could you get the janitor for us?"

The floor nurse sniffed at the room. "Ew, what is that smell?"

"Small accident. Janitor," Olivia repeated and gave a pleasant nod.

"Yes, yes, I'll notify him we have a cleanup." The nurse's head darted away as the door closed.

Olivia turned to Viktor in a wobbly state. "What have I done? I can't believe I just did that. I've never had to harm a person like that."

"You did what you had to do. You knew full well what was in store for you if you had followed her," he said, his calm voice carrying her to relief.

"Thank you, Viktor, thank you. That was quick thinking," she said.

His half smile hidden by the bandage returned. "Thank you. You have given me more peace of mind than you know. You could have had it all—the treasure, a long life—why turn her down?"

"She was evil. I just left one bad person; I deserve better than to run and find another."

"What will you do with the waters?"

"Me? They're not mine—they're yours."

"I am a dead man soon, not for this world. The waters need to be cared for, looked after, something I cannot do."

The question puzzled Olivia. "I'm not sure. I had not thought about the waters." She placed her hand on his cheek and asked, "Would you like another chance? Another life? I could give you a drop of life, set you in the maternity ward, give you the chance at a real life, make up for the one Morgana took away from you."

"No, no, I have had enough. I am tired, I am old, and I am dying. There is nothing left here for me. I have wondered if the water of death might not be better in the last few hours, quick and over. Before I go, we can call my lawyers, change my will. You could still have everything. There is still a chance for you."

"I don't know what I would do with all that wealth, what I would do with all the power, all the responsibility of the waters."

"You could do whatever you want. Help shape the future, invest in medicines, hospitals, worthy causes, and better humanity in the name of Viktor Erikson. There is only one condition."

"What is that?" Olivia asked.

"You must not carry bloodlust. You cannot let the evil infect you like it did Morgana. Remember, being good at thing has nothing to do with it. Being able to live with a thing is everything." He looked at her with an expression of satisfaction. "Stopping Morgana was the right thing, killing her was the only way, but you cannot let that go to your head. Do not kill again."

∽ 30 ∾

Good

Year 2053
Olivia age 26
Viktor age 15 months

WAKING FROM THAT night's sleep felt rewarding. Similar to mornings when daylight savings provided an extra hour in the fall, Olivia woke refreshed and fulfilled. Baby Viktor had his nanny, was safe, and was occupied. She could smell that someone had been preparing breakfast.

After showering and dressing, she made her way to the kitchen where the true treasures of life, fresh bacon and coffee, were warm and ready for her. She felt blessed to be alive, to have a home, and to have a job. There was nothing that she wanted, nothing she lacked. She knew that this was a fortunate time and she should try to linger and enjoy it while it was possible. In a few weeks, maybe months, baby Viktor would start to speak. They would need to have a conversation as best as they could about this situation.

Viktor had been insistent after Morgana's demise to call his legal team. They arrived in the middle of the night, surprised at his condition. No one had actually notified anyone of the accident that took place. Olivia assumed that many may have called Morgana as a contact to let her know about Viktor's condition, the incident, and the few hours that remained. This had been part of her design and plan, to know but not tell anyone else until after his passing—a point when the legal team could not take action, medical specialists could not be called in, or possibly a trusted unknown person could not administer a vile of special water only that person and Viktor knew of. Olivia would not have put it beyond Morgana to have been the driver of the vehicle that hit Viktor that night and sent him to the hospital. She may have walked away from the scene of the crime thinking he was dead or that his body would not be found until much later. These questions might never be answered and were, frankly, details Olivia did not entertain with any regularity.

The conversation with baby Viktor, however, did stay at the front of her mind. A conversation when she would have to explain that after all of the goods and property were signed over to her, the responsibility and trust in her care and ownership, Olivia still went against his wishes and gave him the water of life.

Olivia was one who understood the suffering of life. She had watched it fade from patients' lives only to be pounded, shocked, or injected back into them with violent results. Some did not want to suffer. Many did not want to prolong a life in a vegetated state. The technical nature of being alive and the reality of living were two very distinct things in her mind. Still, she imposed life on baby Viktor after his asking to be allowed to pass. She wasn't sure why she did it other than her belief that he could have a better life, deserved a better life, one of his own.

When she met him in the hospital, he was in a depressed state of wanting to die and not in his right mind. That last part, not being of sound mind, could easily take all of this luxury away in an instant. The cars, horses, acres, and treasures could all go away just as quickly as they arrived, and Olivia was all right with that.

Olivia was very happy at the hospital. She had been offered a full-time position and accepted it. Staying on the estate allowed her to save nearly all her paychecks, so when baby Viktor wanted all this back, she would be fine.

"Here he is," the nanny announced. She carried baby Viktor into the kitchen's breakfast area. He was such a happy baby, full of smiles and coos. It was hard to believe that if Viktor were unhappy to be alive he would act this way.

Settled in his highchair next to Olivia, he grabbed her finger and shook it up and down to his delight. His bright blue eyes could win any woman's heart. In the other hand, he shoved the little Cheerios into his mouth. Between bites, he would sound out, "Goo, goo, goo."

Olivia looked at her tablet, scanning the details of public satellite of images. "You see this, Viktor? I found a map that was locked away in the house. It was drawn by hand, looked ancient, and included a pyramid on it. I think it is *the* map. We could use it with these images."

Baby Viktor looked at her, chewing on the cereal.

"You see?" She pointed. "This is what that area looks like from the satellite." She moved the tablet closer to him. "I don't think anyone has found it yet. We could go there in a few years when you are older. We could see it for ourselves."

Baby Viktor stopped chewing. He looked at her rather seriously.

"Do you realize all the good we could do with another sample of this water? We could take all the treasure and invest it in research that could cure people, heal people, and improve humanity."

Baby Viktor smiled. "Good," he said. "Good."

To read the final chapter of *The Ethics of Immortality* by Autor Widmor, please visit www.paulmichaelpeters.com, select "Autor Widmor" in the index, and then, when prompted, enter the password: Ponthieva.

Other Works by Paul Michael Peters:

PETER IN FLIGHT

Peter can tell you how to run a great marketing campaign. He can tell you everything there is to know about successful trade show programs. He can tell you stories about the thousands of people he has met, miles he has flown, hotel rooms he has stayed in, and ways to work the system to your advantage when you travel. But he can't tell the woman he loves how he feels. Think *Up in the Air* meets *Planes, Trains and Automobiles*. Based on his own extensive business trips, Paul Michael Peters brings us this funny, bittersweet story of a traveling software salesman. Filled with wry observations and entertaining vignettes, life moves fast in this quick read about a "trade show guy" and a love he thinks he can never have.

THE SYMMETRY OF SNOWFLAKES

It's the day before Thanksgiving, and twenty-nine-year-old business owner Hank Hanson is about to tackle the annual challenge of visiting every one of his relatives. The product of a blended family, Hank has parents, stepparents, and former stepparents—not to mention an assortment of siblings—and feels the responsibility to see them all.

To give structure to his unconventional network, Hank compares it to a snowflake's intricate design. The only missing piece in his life, the element that would form that rare, perfect snowflake, is the love of an amazing woman.

When Hank meets Erin at the Thanksgiving Day parade, it seems like she might just be that woman—until pressures start to mount with his family and business, and secrets about Erin's past spill out.

MR. MEMORY AND OTHER STORIES OF WONDER

Uttering the name Mr. Memory evokes the live performances and talk show appearances when he would impress the world with his abilities of recollection. His clarity of remembrance has kept listeners captivated for days while sharing the adventures of his life. In this collection of short stories, we learn the truth about Mr. Memory, the fantastic gone unseen, and a world of wonder which can inspire us to believe.